STRAY

AN ANIMAL AFFINITIES NOVEL

ANGÉLIQUE JAMAIL

MEMENTO VIVERE PRESS

Stray

Developmental editing by A.C. Bauer
Copy editing by Ynes Freeman
Print manuscript formatting by A.C. Bauer
E-book formatting by A.C. Bauer

This book is a work of fiction. The characters and events portrayed are a product of the author's imagination. Any resemblance to real people or events is coincidental.

Publisher's Cataloging-in-Publication Data
Names: Jamail, Angélique.
Title: Stray / Angélique Jamail.
Description: Appleton, WI : Memento Vivere Press, 2026. | Series: Animal affinities; book 2. | Audience: Ages 16-18. | Summary: A teenage girl navigates changes in her friendships, family relationships, and dating when her animal affinity emerges.
Identifiers: LCCN 2026933944 | ISBN 9781964501086 (pbk.) | ISBN 9781964501093 (ebook)
Subjects: LCSH: Teenage girls – Fiction. | Interpersonal relations – Fiction. | Human-animal relationships – Fiction. | Coming of age – Fiction. | Houston (Tex.) – Fiction. | Beirut (Lebanon) – Fiction. | BISAC: YOUNG ADULT FICTION / Coming of Age. | YOUNG ADULT FICTION / Magical Realism. | YOUNG ADULT FICTION / Fantasy / Dark Fantasy.
Classification: LCC PS3610.A43 2026 | DDC 813 J-- dc23
LC record available at https://lccn.loc.gov/2026933944

ALSO BY ANGÉLIQUE JAMAIL

THE ANIMAL AFFINITIES SERIES
A Narrowing Path

POETRY
The Sharp Edges of Water

DEDICATION

for my own Taita (1922-2001):
I'm so grateful to have her recipes and for the hours
I spent learning to cook with her

for Aaron:
because every book I write is also for you

for everyone else who needs to read this:
I see you
You matter
You are necessary

Author's Note

WHILE MOST OF THE names in this book will be easy to pronounce, I want to give a quick guide for two of them because they are Arabic names and might not seem to necessarily follow the usual English conventions for pronunciation.

Raqia should sound like "RAH-kee-uh." It is widely considered a Muslim name with Urdu origins, but there are certainly women with this name who don't identify with either Islam or Urdu.

Taita should sound like "TIE-Tuh." It is a term in Lebanese Arabic (and perhaps also in other dialects) which means grandmother, but which also has affectionate connotations. Unlike in English, where a second instance of a consonant sound might be somewhat muted, both "t" sounds are specifically pronounced. In my family, multiple grandmothers are all called Taita, but with their first names given to distinguish them; for example, I called my grandmother Taita Rose and my great-grandmothers Taita Mary and Taita Liz. This word is also frequently spelled "teta" or "tita," but I have chosen the spelling "taita" to help distinguish it from other languages where "teta" and "tita" refer to different familial relationships.

An additional endearment in Arabic that is used often in this book is *habibti*. This is pronounced "ha-BEEB-tee" and is the feminine form of the more commonly known *habibi*. This word means "sweetheart" or various variations on that and can be used in a variety of contexts, including to indicate close or affectionate familial and friend relationships, in addition to romantic ones. The context matters. For example: I often call my children "Habibi"; I called my grandfather when he was alive my "Habibi"; I refer to one of my dear colleagues who is also Lebanese as "Habibti"; I had a pet in middle school I named "Habibi"; and I've used this name with my cousins and other close friends, and of course my husband. And all of those relationships are different, and this endearment in all of those contexts is correct.

I

W ALKING HOME FROM SCHOOL on Thursday, Raqia tells her best friend Anabelle, "This week has been stupid long."

Anabelle nods. "As long as a swan's stretched neck." She knots her blonde ponytail into a bun and shifts her backpack to the other side. "Lord Jesus, I'm so ready for the weekend."

It's the end of September in Houston and the trees are still as green as ever, the sun hot enough to make the girls sweat through their T-shirts. Raqia lifts the thick black braid hanging down over her shoulder and piles it on top of her head to catch the furtive breeze.

"This weather would be so much easier if we were birds," Anabelle continues. She lifts her arms toward the sky and makes graceful, determined flaps as if she might surprise herself by taking flight. "I wonder if we could create our own air currents." She looks at Raqia with a hopeful seriousness. "Do you think the feathers would be noticeable for long? Are they insulating or cooling?"

Raqia shrugs. "Taita told me she had hers for only a few days," she says, referring to her grandmother. "I don't think they last longer than pinfeathers." Then she grins. "And I'm pretty sure she's never actually flown—outside of an airplane."

"Oh, *ha*," Anabelle scoffs, but she can't completely hide her smile. "Do you think you'll have the same affinity she has?"

Raqia shrugs again. Animal affinities are usually too random to run in families very often, and Raqia hasn't shown any sign of hers at all yet, so there's no telling how she'll turn out. Her grandmother's owlish tendencies are no guarantee of Raqia's own evolution.

Anabelle sighs and kicks a small crumble of sidewalk cement into the yard they're passing. "I'm really tired of waiting," she mumbles.

"Yeah." There's no point in saying much else about it. They're both already in eleventh grade, and neither has shown any hints of their selves at all. Raqia knows—they both know—that it isn't unusual to get most of the way through high school before definitive signs show up. So she tries not to worry about it. Yet.

"I've been thinking about signing up for a session with that new counselor," Anabelle says. "The one who didn't find her affinity until really late. Elsa something." She pauses. "Are you planning to go?" Their school's fledgling chapter of Plain Isn't Pain—a sparsely populated club of nobodies—is bringing in some motivational speaker next week. Raqia expects it to go badly. She shakes her head.

"It just feels like almost everyone else at school has found their affinity already," Anabelle continues, shuffling lightly through purple wisteria blooms that have fallen onto the sidewalk.

Raqia nods. She longs to feel grown-up and powerful, confident like those girls who prance around campus, all fluttering feathers in their long hair and strong footfalls in their gait. They know they belong, and where. Nothing can touch them. And that doesn't make the waiting any easier. She and Anabelle are both weary of being written off as Plain Ones.

"It's been a long week," Raqia says again.

The summer is one thing. They don't spend a lot of time around the other kids from school when it isn't in session, so their Plainness—their *presumed* Plainness, Raqia reminds herself—isn't often tossed in their faces. But this August, even more of their peers came back all figured out, their animal natures evident and sometimes on full bragging display. Ready to be considered full people by the adult world. So many of them, it surprised her. Raqia and Anabelle have tried not to call attention to themselves at school so people won't notice their affinities haven't emerged yet. Their efforts have resulted in varying degrees of failure.

As they turn the corner at the entrance into their neighborhood, someone calls Raqia's name from just behind them. A few guys from school are lounging next to and inside a car parked in a driveway there, and one of them, Alain from her French class, stalks up to her. His striking red coxcomb stands up like a scalloped mohawk. Normally he keeps it sandy brown like the rest of his hair, but he's gone full scarlet in honor of the game tomorrow night. He stands quietly in front of her. Raqia and Anabelle look at each other in confusion, but before either of them can speak, Alain crows loudly in Raqia's face, causing both girls to jump.

The other guys near the car laugh, and one—a newly affined manticore, by the looks of his too-many teeth and vestigial scorpion tail—turns around and swishes his stinger at them. Gross.

"Hey, when's your tail finally going to fall off?" Anabelle calls out to him. It's like she's asked him when his testicles are going to drop.

"Maybe it won't," he calls back, then makes a lewd gesture. "I'll bet you'd like that."

"Wow, ugly *and* stupid." Anabelle rolls her eyes and turns back to Raqia, who wants to exit this situation fast, but doesn't want to look like they're afraid of their classmates.

"Don't insult my boys, you Plain little blonde freak," Alain says, his voice rising.

Raqia clocks the brief flash of worry in Anabelle's eyes and takes one tiny step in front of her. "Hey, Alain, it looks like you're growing a wattle." She points dismissively at the uneven beard under his chin, also dyed red for this weekend. "You should maybe get that checked out."

He then volleys a word at her she doesn't know, but his inflection and sour expression tell her it isn't meant to be flattering. He says it amid a string of advanced French that includes *Liban*, the name people use to refer to when Lebanon was under colonial rule. She knows enough about history to feel insulted. Alain's attitude unnerves her, too. A couple of the other guys snicker and one gives a low whistle. Anabelle doesn't speak French at all and looks around uncomfortably.

Alain lifts his angry eyebrows at Raqia in challenge. *"Et alors. T'as quelque chose à me dire?"*

She translates in her head as quickly as she can. *So then. You have something to say to me?* She wants to tell him off, but she doesn't speak French—or, frankly, Arabic—well enough to do it in either language with real confidence, and in English, her comeback might be parroted back at her by his friends for weeks. Still, she tries hard to remember how Taita had once told an obnoxious telemarketer who wouldn't stop calling their house to piss off in Arabic.

"Oh, look." Anabelle snorts into the awkward moment of silence. "The French kid can speak French. So what? If you really wanted to challenge yourself, you'd learn Mandarin. Or whale song."

One of the guys standing by the car laughs at that, too. Alain takes a step forward toward Anabelle. A woman comes out of the house and calls, "Louie, your maman rang. It's time for you to come home." The guy who laughed snickers at Louie, too, who groans loudly and rolls his eyes from the passenger seat.

"Let's just go," Raqia mutters, pulling Anabelle by the arm and pushing past Alain, annoyed that she couldn't think of anything better to say. After a few steps, she glances back over her shoulder.

He's walking back toward the driveway. Louie has emerged from the car; he sports painted red tiger stripes across his bulky arms and is kicking the gravel trench along the edge of the yard. Another guy has spiked his hair into horns. When Alain reaches them, preening and strutting, they high-five and whoop like the zoo exhibit they are.

Tomorrow night is homecoming, and the mania surrounding the football team is nauseating. Raqia and Anabelle keep walking. Alain and his friends don't follow them.

So yeah, Raqia is ready for the weekend, but she's maybe even more ready for next week, when all of the primate frenzy about this game will be over.

She and Anabelle finally reach Raqia's house. A sign hangs from the street-lamp in the front yard, decrying the loss of a neighbor's platypus. The frantic text offers a hefty reward, but someone has added a sticky note to the edge: "Wolves suspected. Proceed with caution." They look at the sign and at each other, and Anabelle glances at her own house across the street, then looks down at her shoes, waiting for an invitation.

"Want to come in and see Taita?" Raqia asks, just like pretty much every day.

"Wouldn't miss it," Anabelle says with a cheery smile. She likes being specifically invited over. Something about southern manners, she said once; Raqia just rolls with it. It's easier than forgetting to ask and then hurting Anabelle's tender feelings over something that doesn't matter.

When they come through the front door, they find Taita watching a special news bulletin, her face pinched and a half-rolled grapeleaf wilting on the wax paper in front of her. The television is turned up too loud and set at an odd angle so she can hear and see it from the kitchen table. She jumps at the sound of the door closing.

"Taita, is everything okay?" Raqia asks. She and Anabelle drop their backpacks behind the couch and dutifully walk across the room to greet her.

"Oh, yes, habibti, I am fine," she insists, wiping the corner of one golden-brown eye. She gives them each a quick kiss hello and turns her attention back to the food in front of her, her sharp fingernails slicing through the larger leaves to make each one the correct size.

"What's going on?" Anabelle asks, gesturing to the television. A shaky cell phone video shows some aggressive-looking guys scattering outside a store front somewhere. It's hard to tell what's happening: the video zigzags around as the person holding the phone obviously runs from the fray, and the noise of people shouting and cars stopping short—of someone trying to direct people around the area—muddies everything. The news anchor's voice-over trying to make sense of things only adds to the confusion.

"Wolf packs again," Taita answers, pushing her large round glasses up onto her beaky nose.

"Did they say who?" Anabelle asks, biting her lip. "Is it here in Houston?"

Raqia's stomach clenches. This summer, organized packs started prowling around, making trouble in Dallas and San Antonio. It started as pranks, a few busted-up mailboxes and the air let out of a police car's tires. A bunch of young twenty-somethings acting out on their wolfish natures. Shenanigans that are more annoying than dangerous, that have been going on for a few years now. But things escalated when some guy home from college was beaten up—badly—for being Plain, even though it is possible for one's animal affinity to emerge in adulthood. Theoretically. Raqia supposes that counselor coming next week is proof of that.

"They are growing bolder," Taita says, resignation sitting heavily in her throat. "I heard a few weeks ago, some packs have turned up in Galveston and Beaumont. It is like Beirut all over again."

The infamous Beiruti wolf packs, their violence, drove Taita to emigrate, although no one else in the family had been willing to leave. Even Raqia's widowed father stayed behind, citing his important position at the Université Saint-Joseph de Beyrouth. He made no objection to his mother's taking her only grandchild with her. Raqia was three.

"And now they have found wolves in Columbus," Taita continues, waving a moist hand at the television.

"That's still a ways off," Anabelle says, but she looks uncomfortable. Columbus is only an hour and a half away. "And I'm praying every day that it stays a long ways off." But Houston is the biggest city in this region, so it's just a matter of time before an organized wolf pack makes itself known here.

Taita sighs and murmurs softly in Arabic. Raqia knows what that means. Taita left behind family, friends, and homeland to protect her granddaughter from the wolf menace. Once they emigrated, she focused on speaking English to integrate into their new home, so Raqia never really became fluent in their native tongue. And though her own use of Arabic words has lapsed considerably in the last several years, she catches in her grandmother's tone the flavor of a lament, a phrase that suggests they might as well have stayed in Lebanon.

The news anchor describes a litany of offenses the pack in Columbus has perpetrated over the last week. It seems they've graduated from smashing car windshields to robbery. The candid video is back, now that the phone's owner has apparently moved far enough away from the action to get a decent shot, seemingly crouched behind a parked car. Raqia watches the pack fleeing the scene. They have on jeans and black T-shirts from various concerts and wear their hair long and shaggy; they howl and holler to each other as if in glee against a soundtrack of sirens and burglar alarms. The butcher whose shop they've blown over stands in his doorway shouting and waving a cleaver. His apron, stained with the smears of his trade, reads "Joe's Halal Meats."

Raqia's insides churn as she remembers the stories Taita told her about Beirut. She has always taken comfort in the idea that the bad wolves are confined to another part of the world, even while feeling guilty that she doesn't worry if they are in her homeland, as long as they aren't in her home-now. She might feel worse if her father didn't insist, every time Taita calls him, that he is safe. Most wolves aren't the university type.

Suddenly the footage on the television zooms awkwardly on what must be the alpha, from the way he's directing the others. His face flashes across the screen too fast to be identifiable, and the camera focuses on the wads of money he's stuffing into his jeans pockets. He shouts some guttural command at the others then bounds away just before the first police car arrives. Soon an officer comes up to the bystander filming and shuts down his phone. The news report cuts back to the anchor, who introduces an Affinities Behavior Psychologist from Texas A&M University.

"Being a wolf is different from having other animal affinities," this Dr. Crystalle Delacoeur explains. She has golden skin and a wild mane of hair that frames her noble face. "Whereas most people enjoy animal traits that enhance their appearance or senses or even talents, over time more wolves are evolving to become more lupine than human, and the path to that transformation—especially lately, as we've seen—can sometimes take a turn into savage territory."

Anabelle fidgets and begins playing with her hair, chewing on her lip.

"The historical record shows it was not always this way," Dr. Delacoeur continues. "The change began around one hundred fifty years ago but was so gradual at first, the best accounts we have of it are only anecdotal. Perhaps one in a thousand violated the bounds of polite society. The greatest shift we've seen, this trend toward violence, has become more pronounced only in the last generation or so. Preliminarily, we suspect that increased social divisiveness, the growing polarization in politics and other cultural wedges, may have something to do with it."

Raqia doesn't need a psychologist to tell her that people are becoming angrier these days, that the world is growing more hostile. She heard some other affinity behavioralists talking about all of this on a radio program recently, about how the most brutal lupine instincts seem to be following other negative social trends. Gang violence, crime rates, even corporate and political corruption are all spiking in places where the wolf affinity shows the most concentration. But no one has yet offered any reliable conclusions why, at least not that she and Anabelle have heard about.

Dr. Delacoeur's voice again: "The causes for this are still being studied—which makes a good segue into a new research program I'm heading. We're looking for volunteers, people with wolf affinities—"

Anabelle turns the television off. "We don't need her commentary," she mumbles. Taita looks at her with compassion. "I'm just tired of hearing about wolves, that's all."

"You are tired of worrying about them," Taita observes.

Anabelle sighs. "I'm tired of worrying about one of them."

Raqia knows her friend has been watching the news report for one reason: to see whether her brother's face will turn up. It doesn't. Eddie, Anabelle's older brother and only sibling, is the kind of wolf who defies the stereotype: he isn't a Big Bad.

He's actually kind of a sweetheart; he grew nicer as he grew older.

"It's frustrating," Anabelle says. "I can't understand why sometimes I'm worried sick about him, and sometimes I just wish he'd go away and live his own life somewhere else far apart from mine."

Sometimes Eddie and Anabelle get along and sometimes they don't, just like any siblings. Raqia doesn't think this is a big deal—but she lacks brothers and sisters of her own, so Anabelle is rarely inclined to listen to Raqia on the subject. Maybe Anabelle worries their fighting will make Eddie turn Bad?

"This is all just sensational anyway," Raqia says, gesturing to the television. "Plenty of wolves don't turn into criminals. But the normal ones with normal lives don't make it onto the news."

Taita clucks under her breath and turns back to her grapeleaves. "I do not know, habibti, I do not know." She sniffs and gestures toward the television. "These wolves today are not like the wolves I knew when I was your age. Back then, a wolf and a lamb could still be friends." She's quiet then, and Raqia knows she's thinking about the spree of pack violence that led to the deaths of many Beiruti citizens, including Raqia's mother. It's not something they discuss, but that tragedy is never far from their minds when wolves make the news.

A few years ago, when reports broke of the first pack on American shores, Taita lectured Eddie soundly about pack wickedness, but he swore nine ways to Sunday that he wasn't involved in any of that. Taita has known Eddie for years, ever since elementary school when he and Anabelle started spending most of their free time at Raqia's house. Otherwise, Taita might have banned him from her home when his affinity showed up.

And because Raqia has grown up with only stories and not many conscious memories of Lebanon, Beiruti packs or otherwise, she feels more confident about Eddie than the wolves who turn up in the news reports.

So she puts an arm around Anabelle. "*Some* of the wolves have turned bad, but some definitely have *not*." She waves dismissively at the television. "Nothing about those guys means anything for anyone else."

Her friend hugs her back. "It's like I keep telling Eddie," she says. "Pray away the prey."

Raqia gives her a half-hearted nod at the platitude; she doesn't think prayer is going to stop a wolf's predatory instinct, but there's no shaking Anabelle's newly intense faith. She herself would feel better if science could figure out why the wolves are changing.

They join Taita in the kitchen.

"Can we help?" Raqia asks.

Taita swivels her head around to smile at them. "If you like," she says, but Raqia knows this politeness is just a dance she and her grandmother perform. Of course well-behaved Raqia will help, and because of this, so will Anabelle. After washing up, the girls sit at the table and pull sheets of wax paper and a short stack of grapeleaves in front of them. Taita long ago taught them how to roll an inch or two of raw lamb and rice into a tender leaf, to wrap it tightly so it won't unravel in the boiling pot.

"How was school?" she asks.

Raqia shrugs. She doesn't want to tell her grandmother about the rando bully who was a disparaging jackass to her and Anabelle in the lunchroom. Anabelle came back from gym class a little dewy, and when her moist hands left prints on the table, he slug-shamed her and loudly commented that he was going to start carrying a box of salt with him. "It was fine."

"Homecoming is tomorrow," Anabelle says, blushing as a smile replaces her worry over the news report.

"Ah, I had forgotten!" Taita clucks. "Homecoming—I never did understand. How are the football players coming home? Whose home are they going to?" Her grin is subtle. "It never made sense to me."

Raqia and Anabelle both groan at the old joke. "You know that's not what it's about, Taita!" Anabelle says, her hands pausing mid-roll. "It's just a name. The alumni are coming home to watch the game."

Raqia didn't know that was the idea behind the word, though she has always liked the sound of it. "Homecoming" calls to mind permanence and predictability. Something a person can depend on being there when they need it.

"Are you girls going to the game?"

"Nope," Raqia says. Eddie was starting quarterback all four years of high school, and Anabelle was required by their parents—their dad, mostly—to show up when he was playing. She insisted Raqia go, too, to keep her company, even though neither of them likes football. It's just a bunch of loudly grunting boys crashing into each other, proving how rhino they are, no matter their affinities. Raqia hopes they can spend their Friday nights doing more fun things now that Eddie has graduated. She has visions of movie nights and pedicures and taking silly magazine quizzes instead of getting a sore bottom from sitting on cold metal bleachers for several hours.

"We're definitely going to the dance Saturday night," Anabelle says, smiling, her mood improving by the minute. "Taylor asked me to go out to dinner at Franco's and to the dance with him."

Oh, Taylor. Anabelle's crush, the one taking her to homecoming, the one guy she's ever liked who doesn't seem to mind that her affinity hasn't come out yet. He's a decent guy.

"Ah," Taita says. "Franco's is very nice."

Raqia gives her grandmother a sly grin. "She hasn't been this excited since Eddie left for college." Anabelle's even willing to forego her volunteer shift at the animal shelter Saturday afternoon so they can get ready together. Raqia will go out to eat with Taita and meet up with Anabelle and Taylor at the dance later, since she doesn't have a date herself. There's no one at school she would want to go on a date with, even if someone in her grade were interested. Which they aren't. Which is fine, really. She thinks about Alain and his coterie. Who would want to go out with boys like that, anyway? She's happy for Anabelle, though.

When they finish rolling the grapeleaves, Taita carries them to the enormous pot on the stove and drops them carefully in, then covers them with water and lemon slices, then finally a ceramic salad plate to keep them from coming unraveled as they boil.

"Do you want to stay and have dinner with Raqia?" she asks Anabelle.

It's Thursday, which means Taita will be going out for the evening. She has her own social group of other Lebanese ladies, older women who meet every week for bingo or card games. Sometimes they have dinner and talk about their grandchildren. And when one of them is terribly ill or has a death in the family, they all come together to make food for the family who needs it.

The Lebanese diaspora is vibrant in Houston, but Raqia has always felt out of place in it without fluency in Arabic and without a large family.

Anabelle shakes her head. "Thanks, but Eddie came home last night, and I'm supposed to be there." In high school he was an All-American, and this is Texas, where football is practically a religion. No chance Eddie won't come back for his alma mater's homecoming game.

Raqia smirks. "Hail the conquering hero."

Anabelle looks at her while she washes her hands. "I was hoping you'd come over, too."

"Are your parents also going to be home?" Taita asks, her eyes narrowing into keen circles.

Anabelle snorts. "Oh, they wouldn't miss their favorite boy in the world. They'll be home in time for dinner. Dad probably won't even work late tonight. No dance studio for Mom."

Raqia wonders sometimes whether Anabelle worries so much because their parents seem to worry so little. Eddie can do no wrong in his father's eyes, after he proved himself such an alpha on the football field.

Anabelle looks back at Raqia. "Do you mind?"

And suddenly Raqia wants to. It will make her feel better to see Eddie—fun-loving, friendly, not malicious in any way. The news bulletin has unsettled her. She wants to be reminded that not all wolves are criminals. And Eddie—well, it will be nice to see him. Ask him how college is going.

"I don't mind," Raqia says, then looks at Taita. "Can I go over to Anabelle's house and buffer her from her scary older brother?"

"Rocky!" Anabelle swats her with a dish towel. "Don't tease!" Raqia giggles and snaps her own towel back.

Taita laughs, a throaty sound that shakes her shoulders and feathered, brown-and-gray hair, but it's strained. "Of course," she says, then points to a large platter of grapeleaves she has already boiled. "And take him some of those. He cannot get them homemade up at school."

Anabelle hugs her. "Thank you, Taita."

"But you must get your homework done." The girls both nod. "How much do you have tonight?"

"Only biology and history." Raqia's two favorite subjects. "I've done everything else."

"I don't have much, either," Anabelle says. "Some math, and the same bio homework Rocky has. We can work on it together."

Taita nods. "That will be fine. But come back home by ten, habibti," she warns Raqia. "It is still a school night. And you never know who will be prowling around in the dark."

2

Raqia knows the first thing Anabelle will do when they get to the Fosters' house is try to find her cat. It's the same every time. Anabelle bursts through the front door and drops her backpack immediately; Raqia moves it out of the way so she won't trip and puts hers next to it.

"Chuy!" Anabelle calls in a singsongy lilt. "Where are you?" She checks the chairs in the dining room to see if the cat is hiding under the table. "Meow?"

Raqia stifles a laugh as she goes to put the food in the refrigerator. Anabelle thinks saying meow is like speaking cat and has started doing it ever since Jessika in their math class bragged that her Aunt Lois's cat can understand her when she speaks. Anabelle's efforts haven't produced any results with Chuy yet. Raqia looks around for the cat on her way back into the front hallway.

"There you are!" Anabelle squeals when she sees the animal lounging halfway up the staircase, and she runs to scoop it up in a hug. The tabby grudgingly submits to her affections but doesn't reciprocate. Raqia watches her friend coo at the thing, its tortoise stripes undulating as it wiggles in her grasp.

A few minutes later, Eddie saunters through the front door, dark brown hair grown a little shaggy, tousled, and wearing an old Def Leppard T-shirt that's a size too small. He's followed by four other boys from school Raqia doesn't know well. They're seniors who worship Eddie and his full-blown wolf nature even more than his status as a college freshman, although one of them has less wolf in him than a toy teacup poodle. One or two of them are real dogs, Anabelle sometimes says to make Raqia laugh, but both of them know these guys are confident about where they'll land. As soon as the cat hears Eddie's rumbly voice, it hisses and scrambles away from Anabelle's grip and trips up the stairs as fast as its short legs can move.

Anabelle groans. "Eddie! Why are you always scaring my cat?"

"Hi to you, too, sis," he shoots back, then he bares a smile at Raqia. "Hey, Rocky." He tugs on her braid, gently, and lowers his voice just a little. "Always so very nice to see you."

"Hey, Eddie." She smiles back, then when he doesn't say anything else, she points to the kitchen. "Taita sent over some grapeleaves. They're in the fridge."

"Awesome! Tell her thanks." He grins like a golden retriever and heads off in that direction, his fanboys flanking him. "You guys won't believe how good this food is."

One of them, with windblown black hair and bright blue eyes, hangs back. He puts a boot on the bottom step and leans close to Anabelle. "I'll bet kittens taste good, too," he says with a leering grin.

"You leave my cat alone. It's bad enough you're even in my house," Anabelle hisses. Her long blonde hair seems even paler in contrast to her angry red face.

"Watch it, puppyface," Raqia says and pushes his shoulder back. She doesn't know his real name but knows he has a goading disposition Anabelle doesn't like.

He snorts a laugh and saunters off after Eddie and the other guys.

"I don't trust them," Anabelle says through clenched teeth. "Not any of them. Who knows what they'll do once they aren't worried about getting suspended from school anymore?"

"Puppyface sucks," Raqia agrees, "but Eddie's not so bad."

Anabelle scrunches her nose in response. Having them all in her house must put her on edge more than usual.

Then all the guys walk back through the hallway and toward the front door. "I'll be back in a few," Eddie says, his deep baritone barely audible over their boisterous voices. He stuffs two grapeleaves in his mouth at once on his way out.

Puppyface looks back over his shoulder and blows Raqia a kiss. She rolls her eyes.

Anabelle mutters, "I just *know* one of these days he's going to come home for the weekend and wolf out, and I'm going to walk into my room and find Chuy's bloody guts all over my bedroom curtains!"

Raqia tries not to laugh at the melodrama. "*Wolf out?* What does that even mean?"

"You remember that camping trip he went on, don't you?" Eddie found his animal affinity really early, at the beginning of seventh grade. It was a novelty when he gained the ability to grow a full beard over the span of a weekend in middle school. But then on one of his boy scout camping trips, he caught a rabbit and went a little frenzied when he was supposed to be learning to clean it and dress it for cooking. He tore the thing in half and took a bite out of its raw flank, and for a while most everyone at school gave him a pretty wide berth.

"That was six years ago! And your cat is not a wild rabbit, and Eddie's self-control ever since has impressed even Taita."

Anabelle shifts her weight and sniffs, a sure sign she doesn't have a rebuttal. "Still," she says.

"Maybe if you talked to Eddie about it, you would feel better."

"I don't want to." Anabelle is closing off; Raqia can see it in the hard set of her jaw. So stubborn. "It won't do any good, anyway. He never listens to me."

"I don't think that's true."

Anabelle glares. "Whose side are you on?"

"No one's—there are no *sides* here."

Anabelle sniffs again. "I'll think about it."

But Raqia isn't sure how much she believes her.

Chuy ventures back down the stairs, now that things are quiet again, and Anabelle coaxes him into her lap with a catnip mouse she keeps in her pocket. Raqia knows she keeps it there in part so people at school will think she needs it for herself on stressful days—as if Anabelle wouldn't be broadcasting her affinity from the rooftops every morning if she had one. She's just not usually that subtle.

Anabelle found her ancient cat perched on the rim of a dumpster, his tail in the air and his nose buried in a bag of day-old pastries. She begged her mother to let her bring him home. They took him to a vet, who found the animal to be of mature but indeterminate age despite a youthful attitude. That was twelve years ago. Then three years ago, after Anabelle became super involved in her church group, she decreed the cat might be immortal and renamed him in honor of her new favorite person ever, Her Lord and Savior Jesus Christ. His nickname is Chuy, since that seems somehow less sacrilegious.

Eddie calls him The Immortal God-Cat of Westbriar Drive. And when he really wants to upset his sister, he calls him Lunch. Eddie likes to upset his sister a lot, and conflict-averse Raqia has often, over the years, stepped in to smooth things over between them.

He walks back in, alone this time. Before he can speak, Anabelle says, "Your friends are a problem. They shouldn't be coming over here."

"They're fine," Eddie dismisses her. "It's not like you're going to see them much anyway."

"True, you hardly even live here anymore." Anabelle is putting on her priss and Raqia makes ready to intervene. "It's probably best if your thugs just stay away, since this is still *my* house, and I don't want them here."

"Come on, Anabelle." Raqia's hackles rise at the unfair name-calling. It hits too close. "They haven't done anything to you. Saying they're thugs is a bit much."

"This is my house just as much as it's yours," Eddie says, focused entirely on his sister. The fine brown hairs on his arms stand up. "Technically, it's Mom and Dad's."

Anabelle tightens her grip on Chuy, who mews in protest and tries to squirm away. "You leave my cat alone."

"What? I didn't touch your cat!" His eyes darken. "But maybe one of these days I *will*." He stalks back through the hall and off to the kitchen.

"I just wish he would go back to school," Anabelle seethes. "Everything is easier without him."

Easier, Raqia knows, because she doesn't have to balance her worry for his safety with how much he irritates her. "You know he wouldn't really do anything—he's only trying to annoy you. Why give him the satisfaction?"

Anabelle doesn't have an answer for that and just sits there, huddled into her furious self with Chuy, grinding her teeth.

Raqia has never been able to decide what might be worse: having an affinity that people are afraid of, that marks her as a threat and even more obvious pariah—or having none at all. Every time she or Anabelle has felt doomed to Plainness, Taita has reminded them, one more time, that there isn't a timetable for this. That it isn't unusual to get most of the way through adolescence before one's affinity makes its debut. But their parents all showed their affinities early, and Eddie's being The Wolf from a young age makes Anabelle even more impatient.

Raqia can't forget the desperate vow Anabelle made them swear in ninth grade that they'd remain best friends forever, just so that if they ended up Plain they wouldn't end up alone, too. At first Raqia thought the oath over the top, but when her social life failed to blossom in high school—

Eddie bangs around in the kitchen, still sounding annoyed. He and his sister were close when they were little. And now? Well, he's moving on into the world. People like him, people respect him. He's popular and really always has been. He has done things the people around him consider worthwhile, and now he's playing football for a college that wanted him on their team so badly they gave him a four-year full ride.

Raqia has yet to demonstrate any extraordinary talent at anything. She wants success in her life, not just for herself, but also to show Taita the sacrifices she made to bring Raqia to the U.S. have been worth it. She could make her grandmother proud and get her father's attention by going into an academic field of research, making some important breakthrough or solving some big problem. But she'll need to distinguish herself in some way to locate that path, and so far, despite being as relentlessly well-behaved and as good as she possibly can be in everything she does, there isn't much distinctive about her other than the place she's from.

And even that—when she doesn't speak fluent Arabic—isn't something she feels she can claim with a lot of confidence. She makes solidly good grades, but talented students abound at her school. Raqia is fascinated by zoa-psychology and wants to study behavioralism in college, but no reputable Affinities Studies program will take her if she's Plain.

Not having an affinity is just one more way Raqia doesn't measure up.

The thought of never reaching her full potential is a scary thing, and it's something she and Anabelle share. Raqia thinks that fear might be what has made Anabelle so religious recently, praying the rosary and even novenas, even though her evangelical pastor disapproves of such things. Every once in a while someone stays Plain into adulthood, and they've all heard stories of Plain Ones having it rough; sometimes they can't find good jobs or get mortgages. Raqia is afraid of being lonely and alone, looked down upon for not having an affinity, no matter what else is inside of her. She has often wondered whether Anabelle's weird devotion to Chuy is an attempt to cultivate an animal nature.

Eddie walks back in with a half-eaten loaf of pita from the package Taita sent over. A slip of butter and a light dusting of crumbs smear the edge of his mouth. Raqia smells the warm snack and finds herself hungry. He stands in front of Anabelle, who is still stewing on the stairs with her cat.

"Let go of that thing," he says to her, the heat of *his* anger, at least, dissipated. Now he's just the exasperated older brother again. "It doesn't like being held like that." He takes another bite.

"Let him go, why? So you can *play* with him?"

"No," Eddie says, his mouth full. "It clearly doesn't like you." He sighs through his nose and swallows the bread. "Anabelle, you're going to figure out who you are. I have no worries that you won't."

Her eyes water and she relaxes her grip. The cat stops struggling and darts up the stairs. "Do you really believe that?"

"Of course." He smiles at her. "I'm not worried about either of you." He transfers his grin to Raqia. "I can't wait to see how you both turn out."

"That makes three of us," Raqia says, glad the tension between Anabelle and Eddie is evaporating. It's exhausting.

He looks at his sister again, more seriously. "But that cat isn't going to save you."

Anabelle's face closes up again. "We'll just have to see," she says primly. "You don't know everything."

Eddie shrugs. "Suit yourself." He stuffs the last of the bread in his mouth and trudges toward the living room, where he plops onto the sofa and turns on the television. One of those celebrity game shows is on, where people with hybrid affinities like gryphons and other chimeras compete for charity causes. Within just a moment, though, live coverage breaks of another pack attack, this time in nearby Baytown. The reporter starts talking about the alpha—

"That's not how it works," Eddie grumbles then swears under his breath. He switches the television off again right away, tosses the remote onto the coffee table. Leaning forward, he rakes his fingers through his dark hair, rests his elbows on his knees and his chin on his hand.

Anabelle's phone rings from the side pocket of her backpack, a bouncy dance tune, and she jumps up to retrieve it before the voice mail catches. She smiles, her mood suddenly bright.

"It's Taylor," she says. But their conversation, the part Raqia can hear, doesn't sound cheerful as Anabelle paces the hallway. The glee in her voice peters out into a series of half interruptions and, finally, a mumbled "bye."

She hangs up. "I can't believe it," she says. "He canceled." She plops back onto the stairs. "He found out Eddie's back and doesn't want to come over."

"Why would he do that?" Raqia sits down next to her.

"This is so stupid." Anabelle shakes her head. Her voice wavers. "He said maybe he'd see me at the dance." She leans onto Raqia's shoulder and starts crying, the scent of her frustration, the rapid pendulum swing of her emotions, suddenly pungent and alarming.

Raqia pats her hair. "I'm sorry." Her sympathy feels sharp and anxious.

Eddie walks in. "What's wrong with her?"

"She lost her dinner date for the homecoming dance."

Eddie shrugs. "No problem."

"I think it's a problem for Anabelle," Raqia says. "Look at her."

He smiles and his eyes flicker, two dark stars that suddenly look to Raqia like the whole immense universe. "Y'all can come with us."

"Why are *you* going to the dance?" Anabelle snarks into Raqia's shoulder. "Aren't you a little *grown up* for that?"

His glance lights on Raqia for such a short second she isn't sure she's seen it right. "The guys want me to. What else am I going to do on Saturday night?

Everyone will be *there*." He reaches out and pats his sister's arm. "Come on, sis, it'll be fun. Like old times."

Anabelle looks up, her face a puff of pink blotches. "Old times is not what I had in mind." Raqia thinks about how happy Anabelle was when Eddie left for college. She thought her life was going to start fresh. And Taylor seemed like part of that.

"Raqia, convince her." He looks so earnest. "Please." How can his eyes be so dark and so bright at the same time? She wants to stare at them, but that might be weird.

He says, "Come out with us."

Even though his fanboys irritate her, she hears herself say, "Going to the dance with them won't be that bad." Eddie's look then..it could consume her. That's...different. Raqia suddenly feels too warm, almost flushed. She cocks her head. Has she missed him while he was off at college? Well...maybe. That's...unexpected. "That's, um, really nice of you."

He grins at her. "All right then." She can't look away.

Anabelle, however, groans. "That's just perfect," she says. "Can't freaking wait."

3

I T TOOK ONLY A few minutes for Raqia and Anabelle to become best friends. Or more to the point, for Anabelle to save Raqia from what she imagined to be the loneliest childhood in Texas. They met in the middle of third grade, when Raqia and Taita stopped living lease to lease and bought a bungalow on the same street where Anabelle's family lived.

The day was chilly, and Raqia took her skateboard out to the driveway to get free of the stuffy house and out from underfoot of Taita and the movers.

She was still learning the bumps and cracks of the pavement and hit the narrow wooden divider between two expanses of concrete at a precarious angle. Trying to regain her balance, she accidentally tumbled her skateboard over a mound of bubble wrap that had fallen off the back of the moving truck. The popping sound brought Anabelle and Eddie running out of their garage to see whether someone was setting off fireworks, but it was only Raqia, awkwardly sitting on the concrete, lamenting a skinned elbow and scratched-up shin.

"Are you okay?" Anabelle asked, crouching down to inspect the injuries. Her blonde French pigtails were so long they almost touched the driveway.

"Yeah, I think so," Raqia said, but she winced when she tried to straighten her arm.

"That looks like it hurts," Eddie said. "Do you want us to get your mom?"

Raqia looked down, pretending to be absorbed in her scrapes, but finally shook her head. She didn't have a mom, not anymore, and she didn't remember the one she'd had when she was a baby anyway.

"How about your dad?" Anabelle asked, as if that were the easiest thing in the world to do.

Raqia hadn't seen her father in years. "My grandmother is home," she finally said. "I'll be okay."

"You live with your grandmother?" Anabelle asked, her eyes pinched in confusion.

And why wouldn't she be confused? Raqia had been in Texas long enough to know that most people didn't.

Eddie cleared his throat at his sister with a slight edge in his eyes, and Anabelle looked away. To Raqia he said, "I wish I could live with my grandmother. She's an amazing cook and plays the best card games."

Raqia smiled at him. "Mine too. Canasta is her favorite, but I keep forgetting the rules, so mostly we play Rummy and Go Fish."

He smiled back and gestured toward the house. "Want us to get her?"

But Taita was already busy enough today that she'd squawked at Raqia when she sent her out to play, so she didn't want to bother her. "No, I'll be all right." She stood, but slowly, her left hip twinging from the fall.

"You're bleeding," Anabelle pointed out as she also stood. "Come to our house. We have a first aid kit."

"I don't know..." Raqia hadn't seen which house they'd come from, and she didn't think Taita would like it if she wandered off.

"We live just there," Anabelle said, pointing across the street. "It'll be quick."

Her friendly smile made Raqia feel better, so she nodded and let them help her over to their house. They took her inside and helped her bandage up her scrapes, then when they found out she was transferring to their school, Anabelle practically squealed with enthusiasm.

"We're going to be such good friends!" she said, and Raqia found herself optimistic at the prospect.

That Monday, Anabelle introduced Raqia around so she wouldn't be lonely at school, and soon the girls became close. Eddie rounded out their trio, although he and Anabelle bickered like hyenas as they got older.

Raqia shepherded Anabelle through every math class from sixth grade onward, and Anabelle was always the first to comfort Raqia any time a bully at school made fun of her exotic lunches or her prominent nose. They forged a shared history of favorite songs and movies, of Saturday mornings at the museum's dino exhibit and Sunday afternoons swimming with the ducks and riding the carousel at the park. Even as Raqia and Anabelle diverged in their electives and extra-curriculars in high school, each of them constantly searching in her own way for a sense of community, they remained best friends. As the ranks of the still-Plain students dwindled each school year, and the collective attitude of everyone else implied those unfortunate peons were pariahs—even to each other—Raqia and Anabelle clung together.

Now in eleventh grade, when so many of their classmates have found their affinities and forged corresponding bonds that are deeper than the ones formed by just being in classes or on sports teams together, Raqia understands the value of having one good friend.

4

R AQIA WALKS OVER TO the Fosters' house Friday after school. She's loaded her backpack with fashion magazines, nail polish, scented foot scrub, a salon-quality mani/pedi kit Taita gave her for her last birthday, and enough chocolate and microwave popcorn to choke a camel. Staying in for a girls' night during the biggest football game of the season feels rebellious and exciting. Making it a sleepover adds an extra layer of deliciousness. Maybe they'll order Chinese take-out for dinner, or boba tea from the new café down the street.

Anabelle is there at the door to greet her. Eddie lingers on the edge of the front hallway, a few steps from the kitchen with the near-empty container of grapeleaves in his hand. He's still chewing.

"Have you already eaten all of those?" Raqia asks, surprised.

"Growing boy, that one," Anabelle mutters.

He does seem bigger, actually, even though he's only been gone six weeks. His shoulders are broader, his arm muscles more defined. But not bulky. It looks good on him.

Anabelle turns around. "Are you just going to hover, or what? Don't you have a game to get ready for?"

"I'm not *playing* in the game." He puts the last two grapeleaves in his mouth and chews them quickly. "All I have to do is show up."

Of course, and when he does, people will flock to him like seagulls chasing bread on the beach. *The alumni come home for the game.* Raqia wonders if any of his other teammates have come back this weekend.

But maybe not, if he's not hanging out with them. Suddenly his trip home seems…lonely.

"And yes, Rocky, to answer your question, I have eaten all of them. They were delicious."

"I think it took you less time to eat them than it did for us to make them," Anabelle grumbles.

He gestures to the empty container. "Y'all made these?"

"We helped roll them," Raqia says.

Eddie grins at her. "Then they were *extra* good."

Anabelle rolls her eyes at that. "Come on," she says to Raqia, "let's just go upstairs." She starts to head up.

Raqia smiles back at him and has the sudden urge to make *all* the food for him, just because he likes it. She shakes her head at herself and follows Anabelle. Eddie takes the empty container to the kitchen; she hears him rinsing it out before Anabelle closes her bedroom door after her.

Raqia begins taking her girls' night supplies out of her backpack. Anabelle giggles. "Wow, you went all out!"

"Well, we have to do our nails before the dance tomorrow." Was her enthusiasm for girls' night too much? Has she hyped it more than she should have?

Anabelle looks through the stack of magazines and picks out two. "Oh, cool, I haven't seen these yet."

Raqia grins to herself. Maybe not. Maybe it's all fine.

"We're going to have the house to ourselves almost the whole evening," Anabelle says. "Mom and Dad are going to the game with Eddie."

Not surprising. By the time they've figured out what they want to order for dinner, Anabelle's mood is as cheerful as Raqia's.

Before her family leaves for the game that night, Anabelle makes a grudging peace with Eddie and his absolutely unbridled enthusiasm that they'll be going with him and his friends to dinner and the dance, but she spends some time hassling him about it first.

"Who goes to a high school dance when they're in college?" she asks.

He just shrugs. The quiet way he responds, without getting angry at her, makes the girls wonder if he's really having as fun a time in college as he lets on to his friends still in high school.

Later, as their nails are drying while they watch some cliché teen vampire movie—the name of which Raqia has already forgotten—Anabelle admits, "I mean, I guess it's better than staying home all night, moping."

"What?" Raqia tests the stickiness of her big toenail to see if the polish has dried yet. She puts another handful of popcorn into her mouth. The two of them are draped across the sectional couches in the Fosters' den. "This doesn't feel like moping, even if the movie isn't that good."

"I mean tomorrow. Going to the dance with Eddie and his fanboys."

"Sure." Raqia smiles at her, just glad that Anabelle is starting to see the bright side of things. She nestles down into the cushions, starting to feel more excited about the dance now that she knows Anabelle is coming around.

Then it occurs to her: will Eddie bring a date? Something about that unsettles her, but she doesn't want to examine it too closely. Probably he won't, anyway. None of his friends who have been hanging around this weekend are girls.

But then Anabelle goes quiet again, focused not on the movie but on some invisible stray smear of nail polish on the side of her finger. For a solid minute.

"What?" Raqia asks. "Something's on your mind. Just say it."

Her friend doesn't make eye contact. "I just think it could be worthwhile to see that new counselor coming next week." Before Raqia can protest, she adds, "Jessika said she's friends with her Aunt Lois."

Jessika isn't even one of their friends, just a classmate. They don't know her Aunt Lois from an antelope. Raqia sits up. "That's not the ringing endorsement you think it is."

Anabelle shrugs in exasperation.

"What do you think will happen if we go?" Raqia asks quietly, laboring to keep the annoyance out of her voice. "Because I think there are going to be a bunch of pigheaded jerks at the talk she gives, and the minority of us who haven't shown our affinities yet are going to be heckled or catcalled in the halls all day."

"But Elsa got hers so late in life."

"Which we already know is a thing that happens—"

"Even if it doesn't always feel that way," Anabelle interrupts, then sighs, flopping back down on her couch. "Look, I know it's depressing to think about—"

"Anabelle." Raqia leans forward and puts a comforting hand on her friend's shin. "We're still in high school." She draws on every reassurance Taita has ever given them to infuse her words with the specter of confidence. "We're not the only—"

"Plain ones?" A biting edge to Anabelle's voice causes Raqia to draw her hand back.

Raqia doesn't like to think of them as Plain. It feels too resigned. After a pause, she says, "I'm just not sure what you think going to see her will accomplish."

Anabelle goes quiet again, her brow creased, her eyes dark. Grabs another handful of popcorn and chews it carefully, thoughtfully. Exaggerates her movements as if methodical, strategizing. It's a defensive posture Raqia has seen many times before. But then Anabelle sags back into the couch and sweeps her eyes up.

"I just thought it would make me feel better to go talk to her." Her voice is small, fragile.

Raqia nods, resigned. Maybe it won't make much of a practical difference, but if it makes Anabelle *feel* better to go, then maybe there's no great harm in it, either.

"It's fine," she says. "I'll go with you." There'll be a lunchtime presentation sponsored by the Plain Isn't Pain club—and they'll probably all fit inside one regular classroom because who outside of that little club wants to gloriously out themselves?—and then students can sign up for one-on-one or small group sessions with the visiting counselor. "Put us down for an after-school spot."

Anabelle smiles that angel-faced grin she has and grabs another handful of popcorn. "Thanks, Rocky."

Raqia nods and settles back into the couch. They've missed a lot of the movie during their conversation, but somehow it doesn't seem to matter. The same love-triangle drama the characters were stuck in half an hour ago is still their biggest problem. They watch the rest of the movie in muted relief, occasionally groaning at a dumb line of dialogue. The movie has a lot of bared fangs and a lot of kissing. Brooding ensues. They both fall asleep before the credits roll.

5

R AQIA IS AWAKENED ABRUPTLY the next morning when her and Anabelle's phones start sirening. They're still on the couches in the den in front of the television, now turned off. Someone has come in during the night and covered them up with blankets. Raqia picks up her phone and stops the noise and notices that it's already after eleven. She opens the alert to see what's going on while Anabelle rouses herself.

A particularly vile attack on a liquor store has hijacked everyone's news feeds and set off emergency notifications in a twenty-mile radius of the store. A lone wolf—reportedly still at large—is suspected to be the culprit. When Anabelle sees the alert on her own phone, she begins biting at her nails. Raqia has to stop her from ruining her new manicure.

The Fosters' house line rings in the kitchen. Mrs. Foster answers it and after a moment calls Eddie downstairs. Anabelle and Raqia wander into the kitchen themselves.

Mrs. Foster holds the phone against her shoulder and tells Raqia, "It's Taita. She's calling to talk to Eddie."

Odd, but okay.

"He's not coming down," Mrs. Foster continues. "Did either of you see him this morning?"

Anabelle's eyes grow about four sizes, her skin paling even more than usual, as she whisper-shrieks, *"What?"*

"No," Raqia says. "We just woke up."

But Anabelle is already running upstairs, calling her brother's name.

"Can I talk to my grandmother, please?" Raqia asks, and Mrs. Foster gives her the cordless and glides to the staircase to call for Eddie again.

"Hi, Taita," Raqia says. "Is everything okay?"

Her grandmother's voice sounds both relieved and anxious. "Is Eddie home where he is supposed to be?"

There's shuffling around upstairs. Voices, too, Eddie's sleepy baritone among them. Raqia feels an unexpected urge to find him herself and goes to the bottom of the stairs.

"I think so? Anabelle and I just woke up. What's going on?"

"I am just making sure. Have you seen the news reports?"

"Yeah, our phones went off like air raid sirens. But what does that have to do with Eddie?"

Just then the man himself lumbers into the kitchen replete with messy bedhead and slouchy pajama pants and nothing else. He has a T-shirt in one hand. Anabelle follows close behind him. Raqia hands him the phone and tries not to stare at his well-defined bare chest.

"Yes, Taita, I'm home." He yawns. "No ma'am, I haven't even gone outside yet today." A pause as Taita's hurried voice squawks on the other end, but Raqia can't quite make out what she's saying. "No, Taita, I know that—" Eddie pinches the bridge of his nose and squints like he has a headache. "Yes, it's terrible, but I—" A heavy sigh. "No. I absolutely don't." Then finally, "Dear Taita, how long have you known me? Have I ever given you a single reason to doubt—" He holds the phone away from his head so he can stretch his neck from side to side. The popping sounds are epic.

Raqia can tell he's getting a thorough lecture on the dangers of wolves who make poor choices with their lives.

"Taita," he says, "you know I would never lie to you." A roguish grin. "How would I ever get such good grapeleaves without you?" And just like that, his easy charm has come through the phone and Taita's frantic tone seems calmer. Soon their conversation ends and Eddie clatters the phone back on its base. He drags the T-shirt over his head, his arms through the sleeves.

"What was all that about?" Anabelle asks.

He turns around and glares at them. "Nothing." He takes a skillet out of the cabinet and turns on the stove, then goes to the fridge.

"It didn't sound like nothing."

Eddie pulls out a carton of eggs, a bag of grated cheese, some sausage crumbles, and a few mushrooms, then dumps them on the counter. Slices the mushrooms with unnecessary force. "It was nothing, and before you ask me, too, *no*, I did not bump over a liquor store an hour ago. I was asleep." Under his breath, he mumbles, "I'm also not a fucking criminal."

"We know you aren't," Raqia murmurs, but she feels a little bad that her grandmother called to scold him.

He doesn't say anything else as he cooks himself an omelet. He looks so much older than before. Raqia has spent the night over here and seen Eddie in the morning a hundred times, but there's something much more serious about his demeanor now. Something...almost grim. She wants to reach up and tousle his hair or something, but she isn't sure he'd take it in the friendly way she intends. Nothing will lighten his mood right now.

"Fine, let's just go," Anabelle mutters. "It's clear he's not making *us* any breakfast."

Eddie just snorts and shakes his head. Turns the large omelet over in the pan. Doesn't look at them.

"Sure," Raqia says. She didn't really expect him to share his food with them. "I have to go home anyway." She needs a shower and then Taita is going to help her style her hair. They head back into the den to collect their things. When Raqia has packed everything back into her backpack, Anabelle walks her to the front door.

"See you this afternoon?" she asks. "Right on time, like we said?"

Raqia can't fully account for the trace of worry in her friend's face. Eddie's home; he's fine, he's safe. But Anabelle still looks rattled, more than usual. "I promise." She hefts her backpack again and leaves.

6

ONE OF THE LAST significant phone calls Raqia had with her father happened when she was ten years old. Taita called her to the phone. "Habibti," she said, "your baba is on the line."

Raqia dropped her video game controller and raced to the kitchen. She looked forward to their phone calls, even when they happened so rarely—maybe *because* they happened only two or three times a month.

She began telling her father about how she and Anabelle had both done so well on their spelling tests that they were going to get to participate in the spelling bee at school. He always seemed to pay more attention when she talked about her classes.

"It sounds as if you are becoming very good at English," he said in the same accent Taita had. But what else would she be? She hardly knew any Arabic. She was about to remind him she was very smart, and to tell him how well she'd performed on her last science quiz, when muted voices in the background turned his attention away from her.

She heard him put a hand over the phone and speak Arabic in his own muffled voice, a string of rapid sounds she didn't understand, an intense, interested tone he never used with her. A piece of her bruised heart shriveled just a bit more.

"Who is that in the background?" she asked, a slight tremble in her voice.

"Ah...it is..." He sighed. "So, Raqia, I have what you Americans call a girlfriend."

What you Americans? Why did that phrasing hurt?

"And she has a daughter—"

"How old is she?" Raqia asked, suddenly excited. Maybe this new girl could be like a sister, if Raqia ever saw her father again.

"She is twelve," he said.

"What's she like?"

He cleared his throat. "Raqia, I do not know how much it matters."

A cold tremor passed through her. "Why not?"

More muffled Arabic, the cadences almost angry. A tense conversation that Raqia could hear but not understand, that her father was sharing with her unwillingly and only on the surface.

When he came back, he said, "Put your taita on the phone, please." Then he added, "Good luck at the spelling bee. Your education is vital. Do you know that word?"

Numbly she nodded, then found a squeak of voice. "It's important."

"Correct." Then he said nothing.

She realized he was waiting for his mother. "Oh," Raqia said, "I'll get Taita."

"Thank you." He was quiet again, so she gave the phone back to her grandmother. While Taita continued the rest of their brief conversation in Arabic, Raqia trudged back to her video game, but her heart wasn't really in it anymore.

Taita seemed agitated as she disconnected the call and tossed the phone down. She stared out the window at the backyard for a while before Raqia went to stand next to her. She had so many underformed feelings about that phone call, trying to parse out what it all meant. She couldn't articulate it all, but she knew how it felt: empty, and final.

Taita put her arm around Raqia's shoulders, and she leaned her head against her grandmother's side, and without speaking, they watched a lone grackle pecking at the dirt of the small flower bed, before it flew silently away.

7

S ATURDAY AFTERNOON RAQIA GOES over to Anabelle's house so they can finish getting ready together. They have similar dresses they found one weekend scouring Houston's best vintage boutiques; they wanted something different from the usual bodycon bandage dresses that Taita would never approve of. Their pin-up girl style frocks have halter-sweetheart necklines and full skirts that stop just above the knees. Anabelle's is cotton candy pink, while Raqia's is turquoise blue with a small pattern of dark red flowers.

Taita generously called the dresses "flirtatious and cute," but her shallow smile made it clear she thought they showed off too much shoulder, collarbone, and leg. Raqia likes that her dress isn't too green for her olive skin and complements her almost-black hair. They're both happy with their outfits.

But Anabelle's conflicted emotional state resurfaces as she smooths out the white ruffle around the hemline of her dress.

"I don't know," she says. "I hate being Plain, but it's better than being a wolf. Don't you think so?"

Raqia detects the sour tang of desperation in her voice and pretends to agree.

Anabelle rolls her eyes. "And honestly, that fiasco with the liquor store this morning!" But then she looks worried again and begins fidgeting. "They still haven't caught the guy. It's been on the news all day long."

And now the wretchedness of wolves is about to become Anabelle's compulsive topic of conversation for the rest of the evening. Raqia stops her from biting her fingernails right off, but only barely.

"Look," Raqia finally says, buckling her dressy heels on, "it's not that I don't agree, being a wolf isn't fabulous. But seriously." She stands right in front of her friend and makes her look her in the eyes. "He is your *brother*." She wants to add, *Don't you know what I would give to have a brother? Or a sister? Or any family besides a grandmother and a father halfway across the world?* "He's not a bad person. He's not a bad wolf. I don't care what the scientist of the day is saying on the hourly news reports. They don't all turn. They just don't."

Anabelle's eyes screw up and she pushes out an exasperated sigh. "I guess we have to believe that, don't we? I sure hope other people do." She shakes her head. "People who *know* Eddie, they know he's all right. But what about the ones who don't? The news is so awful lately. I mean, what if he just gets picked up by the cops for being in the wrong place at the wrong time? What if he gets arrested just for driving while wolf? It can be dangerous for him even if other people *imagine* he's a threat." She fiddles with a trio of lip glosses on her vanity table. "I just don't want anything bad to happen to him."

"Neither do I."

Anabelle is quiet a moment, then says, "I argue with him too much, I know." She looks up as if searching for help. "He just sets me off. I don't know how not to let him irritate me. I don't know how to—" Her words falter.

Raqia sighs. "I don't think his fighting with you will turn him into a Big Bad, if that's what's worrying you." That just wasn't *him*.

Anabelle looks unsure about that but then shrugs as if to slough off their tension. "Well, we're not going to solve this problem right now." She puts on a wan smile. "We have a dance to get ready for."

Raqia nods but knows they are only putting it aside for the moment.

They're both still applying their make-up when Eddie's footsteps clomp down the hallway and he bangs on Anabelle's bedroom door. She puts her head in her hands and mumbles, "I'm not ready for him yet." Then she calls out, "Go away, Eddie."

"No."

"It's not a big deal," Raqia tells her, closing up her mascara and selecting a lip crayon from her make-up bag. "We're already dressed."

"Fine," Anabelle says. She darts around to find her cat, then picks him up and holds him to her chest. "Come in," she calls, her voice strained as Chuy struggles to escape her vise-like embrace.

Eddie bursts through the door—then stops short. "You two match." The look on his face suggests he doesn't know what to think of that.

"What do you want?" Anabelle scowls as Chuy bats at her neck, paws tangling in her hair.

"I brought you these." He holds out two large magnolia flowers, one for each of them. The stems are freshly severed, still smell like the tree in their backyard.

"Aw, that's sweet," Raqia says. A smile wells up from inside her; she doesn't even care that there isn't any way she can wear the thing. The lemony bloom is the size of her face and looks like suede. She's careful not to touch the petals so their creamy beauty won't turn brown.

"Last of the season," he says. Raqia notices he's shaved, again.

"Thanks," Anabelle mutters. She has to let go of her cat to take the flower, and Chuy scampers off into the hall.

Now Eddie looks pointedly at Raqia and her thick cascade of waves. Taita helped her style her hair like a 1930s screen siren. "No braid tonight?"

She grins. "Do you like it?"

He just nods slowly, his expression guarded. Does he really like it? She can't tell. He stares at her a little longer while she colors her lips, and then he turns toward the mirror on the back of the door, straightens the emerald silk tie he has loosely knotted around the open collar of his crisp navy dress shirt. He tucks his longish hair behind one ear; it's just a little neater than usual. Polished and rakish. The combination looks...good.

Anabelle blots her pink lip gloss as she slips on her heels. When she stands, she wobbles.

"Are you nuts?" her brother asks her reflection, his extra niceness suddenly evaporating. "Your shoes are six inches tall! How are you going to dance in them?"

"They're only four-and-a-quarter," she snaps back as she clasps on a necklace with a gold cross pendant. "And who knows if I *will* dance, since you scared off my date."

"No great loss there." He turns back to face her directly. "You shouldn't be going out with some dumb bunny weakling. If he's not man enough to be around your brother, you're better off without him." Then he looks at Raqia. "No mousy boys vying for *your* attentions tonight, are there?"

As if, she thinks but just shakes her head. He keeps looking at her, though, lips slightly parted like he wants to say more, but he's quiet. One inhaled breath from speaking. Still.

Then the doorbell rings. Anabelle glares at Eddie as she stalks shakily past and down the hall. He smiles at Raqia, who breaks their gaze as she falls into step close behind his sister, ready to put out her hand if needed. Anabelle is liable to break an ankle tonight, assuming she even makes it downstairs.

"You look like a newborn giraffe," Eddie calls out.

Anabelle spins dangerously around, her eyes wide with a mixture of hope and annoyance. "Really?" she challenges. He just shrugs. Her eyes narrow and she turns back to continue down the steps. Raqia shoots Eddie a warning look—she doesn't want to play referee tonight—and he holds his hands up in a "who, me?" gesture.

Their mom is letting a small group into the foyer. Three couples, some of Eddie's friends from Thursday afternoon and their girlfriends, file in next to Puppyface, who already stands waiting by the entrance to the dining room. The boys make woots and hollers at Eddie, calling him "The Wolf" as he descends the stairs with his cocky grin.

"Oh, yay," Anabelle deadpans. "The fan club."

"Who even are they?" Raqia whispers to her. She doesn't know them personally other than as the gaggle of Eddie's worshippers.

Anabelle quickly whispers back, "The one in the baby blue shirt is Kiernan, that surfy blond is Mark, and the ginger-haired guy is..." She twists her lips to the side. "He's new. I don't remember. They're all seniors."

While they all stand around in the hall, waiting for Mrs. Foster to get her camera, the boys ignore their dates in favor of chatting up their idol. Puppyface appears to be going stag—no surprise there. He edges toward Raqia, cocks his head and stares at her with those unsettling ice-blue eyes.

Anabelle wedges herself between them. "What's the matter? You seem to be staring at Rocky." Before he can respond, she says, "Quit it. It's gross." Her smile is as pleasant as ice cream after church on Sunday, but her point is clear.

"I can look at her if I want to."

"You do that," Anabelle says quietly. "But if it bothers her, you can be sure Eddie will rip out your throat." She smiles again.

His complexion turns as cold as his eyes, then, and he grudgingly turns back to Eddie.

"Thank you," Raqia murmurs to Anabelle, who squeezes her hand briefly.

She whispers back, "If any wolf packs do turn up in Houston, my guess is his creepy mug will be the first one on the news."

Raqia and Anabelle don't know the other girls, who stand shoulder to shoulder in a defensive line, and they missed hearing them tell Mrs. Foster their names while they were dealing with Puppyface. Their short tank dresses are mostly obscured behind homecoming mums: a particularly Texan tradition that celebrates each wearer's affinity with profusions of fake flowers, craft store decorations, and polyester ribbons streaming all the way to their feet. The mums have to be held up with halter straps around the girls' necks like the world's ugliest aprons.

One of the monstrosities has two teddy bears on it, holding hands and kissing against the backdrop of a gaudy valentine heart—a display inspired, Raqia thinks, by its wearer's small glassy eyes, tiny nose, and rounded ears. One of the other mums lights up with twinkling, colored lights in the shape of a butterfly, and the third's leopard print ribbons all end in tinny bells that clink every time the girl wearing them takes a step and her feet bang against them.

Forget Anabelle's trouble walking, Raqia thinks. She's sure one of these girls will trip on her mum's tails before the night is over.

The butterfly girl rests her hands on her hips and flexes her arms back and forth. "Where's your mum?" she asks, looking Anabelle up and down. The leopard ribbon girl pretends to inspect her long black nails, but she's watching Anabelle out of the corner of her eye.

"Her date couldn't be here," Raqia says, heading off an awkward conversation about their lack of affinity. She nudges Anabelle. "Your cat came downstairs earlier. Do you want to tell him good-bye?"

She gives her a grateful look. "Yes, he'll be sad if I don't." Raqia doubts Chuy will care, but Anabelle's comment seems to deflect Butterfly Girl's curiosity. Anabelle shakily traipses off just as her mom comes back to take pictures.

Mr. Foster's booming voice precedes him into the hallway. "Fantastic game last night, men!" A boisterous cacophony of cheering and chuckling and reliving the favorite plays of the game crowds Raqia and the other girls right out of the hall. Raqia perches up on the staircase. When Anabelle comes back in, she hovers on the edge of the room, unnoticed by almost everyone else. Mr. Foster has one arm around Eddie and another around Puppyface and is telling a story about when *he* was the star quarterback in high school. He's stocky and tall, friendly and still a little imposing to Raqia even after all these years. He seems not to be aware of his size and keeps going on about his glory days. Eddie looks uncomfortable and glances at Raqia, who just shrugs. If Eddie isn't used to this by now, he never will be.

Raqia can't relate.

Mrs. Foster looks like she's having a wonderful time talking to the girls. "I love that you wear the mums all weekend!" she gushes. "It seems a shame to have them only on game night." One of the fanboys mutters in agreement, alluding to how expensive the mums are. Mrs. Foster points to the teddy bears approvingly. "So elaborate!"

Anabelle pretends to inspect her bright pink manicure, but her face is even pinker.

Then Mrs. Foster makes every couple line up for a picture in the archway leading to the dining room. After that, she waves Raqia and Anabelle over. They stand there and smile to be polite, but Anabelle is still miffed about being stood up, and Raqia just feels vaguely uncomfortable, even without some craft store crime scene around her neck. Mrs. Foster turns to her son. "Here, Eddie, come get in the picture with them."

He bounds over and puts an arm around each of them. Anabelle groans but still cooperates. In that moment, all three of them standing arm in arm, Raqia thinks of all the first day of school pictures they've had together in this hallway, and for the space of a shutter click, they're the same kids they were, the camera's flash burning away the tension between them.

As everyone gets ready to leave, Puppyface positions himself next to Raqia, as close as a shadow. She steps away from him toward Anabelle, and Eddie notices. His glance sharpens toward Puppyface as he shakes his head slowly. A subtle gesture, but it's enough; Puppyface moves back.

"You guys have fun tonight," Mr. Foster says, opening the front door. As everyone files out toward their respective cars, he puts a hand on Eddie's shoulder. "Be careful, son," he says quietly. "Dinner and dance, then back home." He glances pointedly at the fanboys.

"Don't worry, Dad." Eddie ushers his sister out the door then turns back. "You coming, Rocky?"

Raqia nods and follows as Mrs. Foster, already seated on the couch in the den, switches the television on in the middle of a loud commercial break. Then Dr. Crystalle Delacoeur's resonant voice echoes into the hallway—another plea for volunteers for that study on wolf affinities in what must be the biggest ad blitz of the season—as the front door closes behind them.

8

BY THE TIME THEY reach the Italian restaurant, Eddie's friends are getting on Raqia's nerves with their fawning over him and their complete disregard of their girlfriends. She has also figured out that Puppyface's name is Luke, but she thinks her nickname for him is better, and the red-haired boy is called B-Cad, short for Bradford-Caddison. She thinks his nickname is an improvement, too.

Julie, Kirstin, and Nala, whose names Raqia learned only once they arrived at the restaurant, seem more intent on making sure they don't get pasta sauce on their mums than actually eating very much. One of them has pushed her plate away entirely, deciding she will have nothing but breadsticks.

They keep to themselves at one end of the two tables pushed together for their large group—seriously, their dates have *zero* manners—and Raqia sits with Anabelle at the other end, digging into some delicious chicken fettuccini alfredo and avoiding any mention of affinities. The guys are making enough noise, clustered around Eddie in the middle of the group—peppering him with questions about college and playing football at that level and whether he's seen any new movies and if his college town has a big concert scene—that Raqia couldn't make conversation with their dates even if she wanted to.

"They look kind of ridiculous," she murmurs, pointing at Julie's intricate ballet of teddy bear versus spaghetti.

Anabelle grunts in response, but then a dollop of marinara sauce plops down onto Julie's mum.

"Oh no!" Nala squeals and begins rubbing Julie's sauce-covered stuffed animal vigorously with her napkin until it looks like a bloody zombie bear.

"You're only making it worse!" Kirstin says, dipping her own napkin into her seltzer and trying to help clean the marinara sauce away. Julie looks like she wants to cry. Mark and Kiernan, their dates, are just staring at them.

"Those mums are a macabre farce. Bet you're glad not to be wearing one now, aren't you?" Raqia says under her breath, and Anabelle giggle-snorts into her cola. "Am I right?" Raqia laughs quietly.

Eddie gives them a sharp look from across the table, but Raqia has had enough. "What, we aren't allowed to enjoy ourselves, too?" The others aren't paying attention, but she keeps her voice quiet because she doesn't want to embarrass him. "Every night doesn't have to be about you."

He looks stung but hides his face behind his glass of iced tea, and she feels sorry for making him feel bad. It isn't his fault he has a lot of friends. Raqia might be just as exuberant if she had a table full of people excited about the things she had to say, too. She would even wear any stupid mum if she were entitled to do so.

As he drinks, Anabelle frowns at them, questions in her eyes, but Raqia just waves the conversation away and goes back to her pasta.

A few minutes later, Kiernan, who had been sitting next to Raqia, gets up to talk to his date, and Eddie switches into his chair so he can sit next to her. Anabelle stands sharply and excuses herself to the restroom. Eddie watches B-Cad and Mark engrossed in their own conversation about B-Cad's upcoming pre-calc test for a minute, then he leans over to Raqia and asks, "If I tell you something, can you keep it quiet?"

"What, you mean like a secret?" Raqia looks around the table; no one else is paying attention to them for a moment. "Was Pup—Luke involved in the liquor store robbery this morning?"

He scowls. "What? No, I don't know who did that. Some jackass giving us a bad name."

"Are you thinking about participating in that study on wolf affinities?"

Now he grimaces. "No, *thank* you. That's not the kind of attention I want."

"Look, I know you aren't the kind of wolf likely to get his mugshot on the news—"

"Seriously? You think I would be involved with that stuff?" He shakes his head. "I'm trying to make sure it doesn't—" He stops himself short. "Never mind. That's not what I wanted to talk about." He lowers his voice even more, so Raqia has to bend close to hear him. "I'm thinking about transferring to another school. There are some stellar engineering programs here at home, and let's face it, even as good as I am, the chances I make a pro roster are zero to none." He flicks a crust of bread off the table. "As if anyone in his right mind would even *want* to."

The bitterness in his tone surprises Raqia. "I thought you loved football."

"I did. And being competent at it made a lot of things easier for me. But I want more."

Raqia snorts into her cola. "*More?* Greedy much?"

"That's not what I meant. More out of life."

Ah. Raqia nods. She understands that feeling well.

He leans closer to her. "Look, I don't want to play for the NFL; I want a Ph.D. and a career that means something. I want a family—and I don't want to be traveling around, chasing a stupid ball, all the time. Science is going to win out over sports. I refuse to be pigeoned."

Just then Puppyface laughs too loudly at something one of the other guys has said and draws the attention of several tables around them. Raqia thinks maybe *he* ought to sign up for Dr. Delacoeur's research study; he seems like someone who would benefit from rigorous oversight. Eddie glares at him until he quiets down, then he murmurs, "I need to be here." Once Puppyface has blended back into the tamer conversation of the table, Eddie adds, "Here. Not in some provincial college town. I want to show the world there's more to me than a wolf."

"So you'd come back home." Raqia grins. "Anabelle would love that."

He rolls his eyes. "Whatever. I have more important things to deal with than her drama."

She feels indignant on Anabelle's behalf, but only a little. Then a more serious thought occurs to her. "If you transfer, you would lose your scholarship." Mr. Foster will be furious.

Eddie nods. "It's a problem," he admits. "I need some time still to figure it out. I feel stuck."

Before Raqia can say anything else, Anabelle is back. "Stuck how?" she asks, sliding into her chair.

Eddie just shrugs and says, "Nothing. It doesn't matter."

"Come on, tell me," Anabelle says. "You told Rocky."

"Just forget about it," he says. Raqia doesn't like the way Anabelle glares at her for just a moment, as if *she* has done something wrong.

"What, are you *his* best friend now?" she mutters under her breath, but Raqia hears it, calling out to her like an alarm despite the din of the restaurant. Anabelle doesn't look up from her food, so Raqia pretends not to notice. She doesn't want to ruffle her best friend's feathers.

Eddie's ears perk up like he heard his sister too, but then he starts making half-hearted jokes with the guy sitting next to him. Otherwise he and Anabelle both seem subdued through the rest of dinner, and Raqia eats every last bite of pasta off her huge plate just to make the meal come to an end sooner.

9

As soon as they get to the dance, the three couples scatter into the streamers and balloons, the boys high-fiving Eddie for some reason on their way into the crowd. One of the football coaches comes up and greets Eddie with some warmth, acknowledging Anabelle and Raqia tangentially, and asks about the team Eddie is playing on now. Raqia looks past the foyer into the dance. Everyone in the dimly lit gym seems to belong together. When the coach walks away, Puppyface, who has been on good behavior for almost a full hour, admits he's been angling for more time on the field and goes after him.

Several more people arrive in the foyer then and file past them into the dance. A couple of girls, seniors Raqia knows only by sight, stop to lavish their squealing greetings on Eddie, who accepts them with friendly distance, holding one at actual arms' length when she tries to hug him. She looks surprised, and when Eddie takes a step closer to Raqia, the girl looks at her as if Raqia were a bug.

"Where's your mum?" the senior asks, her gaze taking all of Raqia in as if through eight eyes. She shifts her weight in a strangely articulated way. It's discomfiting.

And Raqia doesn't know how to answer. Isn't it obvious? She has no affinity and no date to give her a mum even if she'd matured yet—

Eddie scoffs. "She doesn't need one. Those crazy things look absurd."

This catches Anabelle's attention. She focuses on the conversation suddenly, as if she were being left out of something important. "Well, there *was* that enormous magnolia. Not that there was any way to wear it. But who needs a mum when you have a flower as big as your head?" She gives Eddie a pointed look, then shifts it to Raqia, who doesn't understand—Anabelle got a flower, too, after all.

The other senior puts a hand on her friend's spindly arm. "Let's just go into the dance," she says, pulling her away. Too-many-eyes reluctantly walks off with her on those uncannily angular legs.

Eddie is standing so close Raqia can smell, for the first time, the subtle notes of his cologne. Did he mean to imply he was here as her date? *No way.* But the way Anabelle is looking at the two of them...she clearly must be wondering the same thing.

"What?" he asks his sister, defensiveness lurking in his tone.

"That was ridiculous. Raqia doesn't need you to—" Anabelle shakes her head and sways on her shoes. "You don't play here anymore. Let it go."

Eddie turns to face her head-on. "You weren't complaining last year when my popularity upped your street cred." His voice is even but his eyes, fierce. "I think you're jealous."

Anabelle grits her teeth. "Your charm has worn off."

Raqia steps between them and puts a hand on each of their arms. "Maybe you could save this fight for tomorrow? There's a lotta people here—"

"And you don't want me to *wolf out* in front of them, do you." But he's staring at his sister.

Anabelle flinches first, screwing up her nose and eyes. *"Aarrgghh!"* She pivots and wobble-stomps on her toes over to the table with the snacks and begins filling up a green cocktail napkin with Cheez Balls.

"You shouldn't provoke her like that," Raqia says. Her hand is still on Eddie's arm; it feels tense under her fingers, and she pats him gently. "She only digs in."

He puts his hand on top of Raqia's, surprising her, but then loosens up. "I know." He smiles coolly. "Family brings out the worst in us sometimes."

"I wouldn't know."

He doesn't seem to hear her, though, and leads Raqia the rest of the way into the dance. Then he looks back up at his sister, and his grin darkens.

Anabelle is talking to one of their classmates, a guy with longish ears and downy fuzz on his cheeks. Taylor, Anabelle's crush. As precious and non-threatening as can be. *No wonder he's scared of Eddie,* Raqia thinks, noticing that his nose quivers excitedly when he talks. Anabelle has put her Cheez Balls on the table and has a hand on Taylor's arm, smiling and cutting her eyes at him in a way that makes him grin from one outsized ear to the other. Raqia notes Anabelle's trembling ankle and wonders whether Taylor can see it. They make a cute couple. Just looking at them makes her feel optimistic.

"Eddie," she says, leaning closer so she won't have to shout over the music, "don't mess this up for her, please."

"What're you talking about?"

"I mean it." She tries her most stern voice. "I'll be really mad at you on her behalf if you intimidate him on purpose."

Eddie looks down at her in surprise. "Okay, that's fine. I won't go bust up what is, no doubt, an uninspired conversation."

Raqia nods curtly then looks back over at the pair. Taylor gestures toward the dance floor. Anabelle nods, a hopeful smile on her face. He offers her his hand as they walk into the crowd.

"But you have to dance with me to keep me occupied." Eddie pulls Raqia toward the middle of the gym just as the languid strains of a rock ballad begin. The whole place is a dark mix of silhouetted bodies and noise. Occasional colored lights flash across the room, highlighting her schoolmates' enthusiasm or embarrassment. Some whose animal affinities have already emerged, like the captain of the cheer squad in satin tiger-stripe pants, have dressed to emphasize their pride in the idea that they are somehow, now, more mature than everyone else.

But when the other students see Raqia and Eddie, they either gape at them or...give them a wide berth. She tries to parse out what it means that they are dancing together—nothing, of course, no matter how warm and strong his hands feel around her waist—and what other people will think it means. That's another story.

How will it change things for her at school next week, if anyone still remembers after a couple of days? Everyone knows Raqia is friends with Eddie. Or at least, anyone who has ever paid attention to her and Anabelle has seen all three of them together. Will assuming she's here with him on a date change the way people think about her? Will anyone expect Eddie to be interested in someone who might ultimately end up Plain?

She looks around at some of the other couples slow-dancing, at the cumbersome space a few of the girls' mums drive between them and their dates. Raqia feels just as awkward, even though it isn't like she's never stood this close to Eddie before. But dancing this way feels different tonight, when he seems to be acting like her date. But he isn't her date. And yet, as he turns them in a slow circle in time to the music, he draws her even closer. She shakes her head, confused by all of it, including her sudden and disarming urge to lay her head on his shoulder. She can just stay here in this moment instead, pretending she and Eddie, their arms around each other, are suspended in the midway of any ordinary hug. But that isn't really what she wants, is it?

A few students bound over, excited to see Eddie. He smiles, friendly and nice as ever, but doesn't stop swaying to the music with Raqia. One calls him "bunny wrecker" as if it were some incredible inside joke, and Eddie just nods, a weary smile on his face. "I am what I am," he says and shrugs.

Then they're alone again in the middle of a crowd.

"I hate that nickname," he mutters.

This surprises her. He never shied away from his reputation in high school.

"They act like it was fun to break open a living rabbit and gnaw on its raw, bleeding leg. I wasn't even thirteen, for chrissake. I had no idea what to do, how strong that urge would be." He shakes his head.

After a moment, she asks, "Do you ever wish maybe you didn't have your affinity?" The sad—almost...pitying—look on his face makes her add, "Or that you had a different one?"

He shakes his head. "I am what I am," he murmurs, his tone somber, intimate. "The occasional savage tendency and all."

"You've managed to control yourself admirably in the years since that campout," Raqia says, trying to buoy his mood. "I've never seen you attack anything else." She smiles. "Unless you've been hiding it from us, running off to the woods under the full moon."

He actually laughs then, a quiet, comfortable sound. She loves it.

"Hardly," he says.

With Eddie pacified, Raqia tries to keep one eye on Anabelle—at least if she trips on her own feet, Taylor is close enough to catch her—but Eddie turns her so that her back is to them.

"Try to focus on your dance partner." He grins, but there is a thin edge to his voice that catches her attention. His hands on her waist feel strained, as if he wants to pull her closer and holding back is a difficult choice.

Trying to recapture the easy playfulness of their childhood, she reaches up and musses his hair. "Behave, wolf boy." She smiles with a self-assurance she doesn't entirely feel.

He hesitates. "What if I don't want to?" His demeanor is serious, intent. "What would *you* think if I came back to Houston? If I stayed here?" His fingers tighten at her sides just a little, then relax.

If he comes back, if he stays, will their trio form again? Right now, it feels like a lopsided triangle. Raqia wants to turn around and look at Anabelle but can't—and then she decides she doesn't *really* want to. Looking out for her, staying vigilant about her moods, is more habit than anything else. Raqia can say nothing, just hold herself in this halted moment of indecision. Maybe she can just hold Eddie, right now, for this short time, without—

He sighs when she doesn't answer, a soft sound through his nose like a dog, resigned, settling in. His eyes wander around the room as they sway to the most doleful guitar solo she's ever heard.

It feels surprisingly natural, actually, dancing with Eddie. He's never felt threatening, never to her, no matter how much Taita worried about it when his affinity first came out. Even now, when he leans his head down close to hers, when his hands move closer to each other around her back—even now, she feels safe. But Anabelle's conflicted feelings toward her brother have only grown more intense—anxious, erratic—in the wake of all the recent attacks. The three of them have a long history together and Eddie's wolf affinity—and how the world perceives it and him—have already disrupted that.

Raqia had the idea when she was younger that their trio was inviolate. But if she lets her friendship with Eddie slide into something deeper...which, *huh*, right now feels very appealing... Well, that'll change things even more. She doesn't know exactly what Anabelle would say about that, but if she feels left out somehow, it won't be pretty. Raqia can't choose between them and doesn't want to have to. This would all be easier if Anabelle and Eddie got along better.

Eddie's skin smells faintly of cedarwood, like the carved wooden blanket chest in her grandmother's bedroom. Cedar is Taita's favorite scent, and the cedar of Lebanon is the tree stamped on the gold pendants Taita and Raqia wear on delicate chains around their necks. Taita said they were for remembrance; hers is bound up in the memory of home and family. But Raqia's reminds her of a homeland so distant in time and space that her memory of it is shrouded in mountain fog. She feels apart. It's like having one foot in a place she can barely remember and one in a place that hardly thinks of her.

Raqia's only early memory is from right before they emigrated. She attended a tree-planting ceremony with her father in the cedar forest. His university classes were there, too, some sort of field trip. Taita held her while she threw a tiny clump of soil at the new planting. It was a ceremony meant to celebrate efforts to foster new growth in the forest, but now Raqia thinks it feels more like she was burying the dead.

As the song comes to an end, Eddie slows and begins to loosen his hold on her. The DJ unexpectedly spins another ballad and Eddie hesitates, like he doesn't know whether Raqia still wants to dance with him. But she *does*, so she doesn't let go.

"Again?" she asks quietly.

He nods and grins and holds her close. "Yes, please," he whispers, but she hears it. He seems even less tense now. They drift around and see Anabelle and Taylor on the fringe of the crowd, also swaying, in a wobbly euphoria.

"She worries about you," Raqia says, gesturing toward her. "A lot."

"I know she's mad because she's still Plain."

"I don't think it's *just* that." Anabelle wants to keep her brother safe but can't, and she doesn't know if Eddie can control himself. "I think she's scared." And being angry is easier than feeling helpless.

Eddie looks over at his sister and sighs quietly. "Yeah, I can imagine that."

Raqia looks up at him. "Then why pick on her so much?"

"I don't know. It's what brothers do?"

That's an unsatisfying answer. "Big brothers also look out for their little sisters—and not just by interfering with who they're dating." Eddie and Anabelle are the closest thing she's ever had to siblings. "But then what do I know," she adds in a mumble.

When she was really young, maybe nine or ten, she decided one day to adopt them as her brother and sister and proudly announced this to Taita.

Her grandmother laughed, a mirthless, high-pitched screech, and said, "Habibti, they're not really your family, no matter how much you want them to be." Taita patted Raqia's shoulder affectionately, but when she saw her granddaughter's downcast eyes and quivering lip, she said, "But of course, Anabelle is your closest friend, and of course that's *like* family."

That meant Taita was all Raqia really had. She'd never felt lonelier than that day.

Dancing with Eddie, his face so close to hers, the music loud and the lights low, she doesn't feel so lonely. She also doesn't feel especially sisterly. In her heels she doesn't have to reach up very far—she could kiss him, right here, right now. Would he kiss her back? She slows her sway and tilts her head slightly, brings her face even closer to his.

Suddenly there's a loud crash from the back of the gym, and Raqia turns around to see one of the balloon archways has fallen down, a casualty of a fight between a couple of guys. She can't tell who they are, but it doesn't take long for three or four others to join in the scuffle; it looks like Puppyface is among them. Eddie's arm tightens around her shoulders and a low rumble forms in his chest.

She puts her hand against him. "Don't even think about it," she warns. "I don't care how much everyone loved 'The Wolf' on the football field last year; you'll be thrown out if you get aggressive here."

The eyes he turns on her are angry, distant. "You don't know what you're talking about."

"How do you think people will react if a wolf pack turns up in Houston?" she asks. "You may be popular and in control of your emotions, but you're also the most flamboyant beast this school has ever seen." She looks back at the fight. Puppyface throws a punch at someone. She points at him. "And *that guy* is one of your friends." Panic strains her voice; she reaches up to speak closer to his ear. "You were even on the news when you made All-American. Do you honestly imagine you won't be the first person people blame?" She gestures to the crowd of students, no longer dancing, now egging on the fight.

"What college student comes back to his high school for a dance?" He looks intently at her then, but she can't believe he came here just for her, even if a big part of her wants that to be true. "You have a following—the football players all think you hung the moon. Don't try to deny you love the attention."

"They're all full of shit," he growls. "They don't know me at all." But he is holding himself in check.

Refusing to be pigeoned, she thinks. He clearly wants to get involved in the mess at the other end of the room, though. Then Kiernan stalks past them, his eyes dark and his jaw stern, and Eddie grabs his arm, yanks him back.

His voice in his friend's ear is low but Raqia still hears it. "Think first," he warns him. "Who is that going to help?"

It occurs to her that maybe Eddie wants to *curb* the fight, not join it. Maybe if he moves back to Houston he can keep his fanboys in check, too.

Raqia looks back at the melee and is surprised to feel her own heat rising, the hair on the back of her neck standing up. A passel of teachers and the basketball coach are heading toward the boys to stop the brawl. The music has finally stopped.

She glances around, looking for Anabelle and soon finds her holding Taylor's hand at the back edge of the crowd. At their safe distance, he looks entertained, but Anabelle is watching her brother nervously. Raqia gives her a reassuring smile, but when she looks back at Eddie—why is he staring at *her*? Suddenly self-conscious, she rubs her arm and feels gooseflesh.

"The fight's breaking up," she says. He nods, tilts his head at her. The rest of the crowd is dispersing, too, the students wandering around the gym in clusters. Several make their way to the snack table. One of the football coaches has Puppyface off to the side, a hand on his shoulder, keeping him back out of the fray.

The noise of chatter and footsteps and laughter becomes louder than Raqia can stand, then suddenly a few voices sharpen into pinpricks of focus. She can hear the basketball coach and assistant principal reprimanding the two boys who started the fight in the first place. She can hear their weak excuses, the conversation impossibly rising above the swell of everyone else's talking. *He called me a Plain One,* the kid with the cut on his forehead is saying. *He hit me first,* says the kid with the bloody nose. Raqia can smell him, the mess of his face—

She feels lightheaded.

Eddie catches her around the small of her back. "Hang on, Rocky." She leans against him, closes her eyes. Is vaguely aware of his other arm waving.

Then Anabelle's voice, part confusion, part dismay. "But I'm not ready to leave yet."

Raqia swims up through the noise, opens her eyes. Anabelle looks pissed; Taylor hangs back, casting nervous glances at Eddie. "What? Why are we leaving?" Raqia asks, standing straight again—but slowly.

Eddie glares at her. "I'm getting you out of here."

The angry look on Anabelle's face prompts Raqia to say, "I'm fine," but then a tremor in her stomach jolts her still and a wave of nausea hits.

"You look green," Anabelle says, her forehead wrinkling. "Is something wrong?"

Yes, very, but Raqia has no idea what or why. She thinks of a quick excuse. "Too much pasta." Her voice sounds as weak as she suddenly feels. Everything is horrible.

"Come on, home with you. Let's go, sis."

Anabelle looks back at Taylor. "But—"

"Now," Eddie insists, gravel in his voice. He looks down at Raqia. "Taita'll kill me if I don't get you home when you're sick."

Taylor nods rapidly, his nose quivering as if the threat of violence were real. "See you Monday."

"No, wait—" Anabelle says but Raqia sees him back away out of the corner of her eye. As he walks away, Anabelle wails in frustration. "You ruin *everything*," she says to her brother, who ignores her. She puts a hand to Raqia's forehead. "No fever," she says, then opens her tiny purse and holds out a small packet of stomachache tablets. "This will help," she says to Raqia. "Why don't you take them?"

"That's not going to be enough," Eddie says. "She's about to pass out." Raqia lets him lead her out of the gym, his arm steady around her.

"Aren't you even going to try it?" Anabelle insists, but he keeps walking, pulling Raqia along. Anabelle takes off her shoes so she can stomp next to them, but her bare feet can't properly convey her irritation. "Maybe Taylor can take me home instead."

"Nope," Eddie insists, "we're all leaving. Uber's not allowed on campus, and I don't trust that kid to get you home safely."

"But why not?" she whines. Then emits an exasperated noise that makes Raqia feel irrationally angry, though she doesn't understand why.

"Come on," Anabelle continues, "just give me five more minutes." The music in the dance starts up again. "One more song?" She bargains against their sudden departure all the way to the car.

Listening to her makes Raqia feel even worse. *Just. Stop,* she thinks. Maybe she has food poisoning. She's sorry Anabelle has to leave Taylor, but then another wave of nausea roils her gut. She also wants, just a little, to slap her. The urge surprises her and makes her feel even sicker. She clenches her entire body until the churning passes. When Anabelle mutters something about "all this over indigestion," all Raqia can think is, *Whatever.*

On the way home, Eddie takes Highway 59 to save time, weaving through reckless Saturday night traffic and barreling down the shortcut while Anabelle complains.

"I don't see why you couldn't have let me stay at the dance. Taylor could have brought me home."

"Doubtful," Eddie says, his voice low and angry.

"Then you could have come back and picked me up—"

Eddie turns and growls at her, eyes as dark as Raqia has ever seen them. Even she quakes a little at the sound, but then suddenly she thinks she might throw up and lurches. Eddie puts a gentle hand on her shoulder.

"You're going to be okay, Rocky," he says, quiet, steady.

Anabelle starts to protest again. Raqia is ready for her friend to embrace a little Christ-like compassion already.

Apparently so is Eddie. "You can quit bitching any time now," he finally says, his voice even, his eyes focused as he swerves onto the exit ramp and rolls through the stop signs in their neighborhood. Anabelle shuts up. Or fades out.

The darkness around the edges of Raqia's perception grows larger, consuming...

10

RAQIA DOESN'T REMEMBER GOING inside her house or getting into bed. She wakes up in the middle of the night, parched but no longer nauseated. She goes into the bathroom for a drink of water, but when she turns on the light, what she sees in the mirror makes her jump back against the wall with a strangled shriek.

Her skin is bruised. All over.

As her eyes adjust, blue-gray splotches come into focus on her cheeks and neck and arms and chest and legs. Dark, uneven splotches, swirling across her skin. She touches them gingerly. The skin doesn't feel tender. She traces the patterns and finds them to be mandalas. They're more like tattoos than bruises, she realizes, but where in the hell have they come from?

She opens her mouth to call for Taita, but her voice has vanished. She strains her throat, pushing all the air in her lungs out into a hollow, faint scream that sends her spinning into fear. She claws at her skin as the bruises swallow her up, she grasps at the air, clutches at her own reflection in the mirror, then spins and twists off her balance, falling, falling, her throat screaming into silence—

She darts straight up in her bed, sweating and panting and whimpering, the covers tangled around her. Her pillows have been tossed to the floor. She stares at her skin, her perfect olive skin, no blemishes anywhere.

No bruises. No mandalas. No freckles, even. Everything as smooth and soft as ever, but with a thin sheen of sweat. Her body is still heaving from what must have been a nightmare, the most surreal dream she's ever had.

She reaches for her phone to send Anabelle a text. **something weird happened,** she types.

Three little flashing dots indicate Anabelle is typing, then they vanish. A moment later, the dots again, but then nothing. Finally, a text comes through. **are you still sick?**

She doesn't feel nauseated anymore, just unsettled. **I don't think so...?**

The three dots again, then they vanish. Appear, and vanish. *What* is going on with Anabelle?

Raqia texts once more. **call me?**

The response comes less than a minute later. **no thanks. I thought you were my friend.**

Raqia feels stunned. All this because Eddie made her leave the dance early? It's not as if Raqia *tried* to ruin her night—or as if Anabelle won't see Taylor at school. They have three classes together! She types, **I don't understand...**

sure you don't. An eye-roll emoji. **nothing is the same. not anymore. it can't be.**

Bypassing any twinge of remorse, Raqia rockets straight into anger. She didn't mean to get sick, the nightmare terrified her, she's confused about Eddie and what her feelings for him really are, whether he has feelings for her—*she* deserves to be the most important person in her concern, not Anabelle. She looks down at her arms, legs, chest, confirms her skin is normal.

"So weird," she mutters, suddenly so tired. Picking up her pillows makes her dizzy.

She thinks about waking Taita up but can't muster the energy. She should sleep. *All* of this has to be a dream, an insane, sick-person dream. When she wakes up tomorrow, she insists to herself, everything will be normal again. She fades back into sleep in a second.

II

RAQIA SLEEPS SO LATE on Sunday that Taita is already making lunch by the time she comes downstairs.

"How are you feeling, habibti?" she asks, concern tracked across her brow.

"Better than last night, I guess." The dream didn't come back, but that didn't stop Raqia from thoroughly inspecting her body when she awoke for the discolorations she imagined in her sick state in the middle of the night.

The text messages, however, were definitely real. Anabelle's last one is still displayed on her phone; she hasn't sent another this morning, even though Raqia has tried to contact her more than once. "Was I in bad shape when I got home?"

Taita looks up sharply from the shredded chicken and rice she is stirring. "You do not remember? Eddie had to help me get you into your room." She shakes her head and begins folding sautéed crumbles of ground lamb and pine nuts into the dish. "I would have thought you had been drinking alcohol if I did not know you better." She cuts her eyes at Raqia above her glasses.

"None of us had anything to drink but soda." Raqia sniffs the aroma.

"Do you promise?"

Raqia can't mask her surprise. "When have I ever drunk alcohol?" Truly, she has no interest in anything that makes her feel sick and foggy and act like a brainless boar. Anabelle is too religious to touch the stuff, so Raqia never has any social pressure to imbibe.

"I suppose that is true." Taita appears to relax.

"Are you making hashwe?" she asks. Taita smiles and nods. "That smells really good." Raqia's stomach rumbles. "I hope we eat soon."

After lunch, she inspects herself in the mirror before she showers. No markings. By the time she gets dressed and finishes braiding her wet hair, Eddie calls.

"How you feeling today?" he asks, his voice low and serious.

"Okay, I guess."

"Any more...weird symptoms?"

That's an odd question. "Just a totally surreal nightmare." But describing it will sound crazy. "No big deal." Dismissing it diminishes it.

"Okay, well...good." He clears his throat. "I'm glad you're feeling better."

"Yeah." More or less. Better enough. "So is Anabelle really mad at me?"

He snorts. "She'll get over it."

What can she be mad about? And is it the kind of mad that will wreck their friendship? Raqia can't decide whether the situation is more unnerving or ludicrous. She needs to talk to her in person. "Is she home?" Normally she volunteers at her church's food bank on Sundays after morning services. "I want to come over."

Eddie's voice brightens. "Fine with me! Come on by."

When Raqia arrives, Eddie lets her in and follows her upstairs. Anabelle is sulking in her bedroom, holding her unwilling cat and listening to music through her earbuds.

Eddie stands in the doorway and smirks. "She's communing with God over there," he says. "God-music in her ears, the god-cat in her lap. Probably trying to figure out how to be more godly." He leans forward and waves his hand to get her attention. When she looks at him, he says loudly, "You can start by not being a horse's ass to the one close friend who still puts up with you." He looks pointedly at Raqia. "Good luck. I have to pack. I'm heading back to school this afternoon after Mom and Dad get home." Then he disappears into his own room down the hall.

"Hey," Raqia says, sitting on the bed. Her friend just stares at her, doesn't even take out her earbuds. A sudden flash of worry spreads through her, heating her from the inside then making her feel suddenly cold.

Even when they've gotten into arguments in the past, about what music to listen to in the car or what movie to go see, Anabelle has never seemed truly angry. Well, there was that one time last year when Raqia told her she didn't enjoy going to the hours-long services at Anabelle's church, and Anabelle didn't speak to her for three days, until she went back to church and got filled up with Christ's love again, then forgave Raqia for her sinful attitude.

You know what? Raqia thinks. *That wasn't fair, either.*

"I said, hey," Raqia says more loudly, reaching over to pull Anabelle's earbuds out. A miniature Christian rock concert comes pouring out and for some reason the sound pisses her off.

Anabelle huffs and turns her back to Raqia. Chuy tries to scramble over her shoulder to get away, but Anabelle holds firm.

"Why're you upset?" Raqia can feel her temperature rising again. She hopes it isn't a fever. "I'm sorry I got sick at the dance, if that's what you want to hear. It's not like I did it on purpose."

"Yeah, *sick*," Anabelle says.

Raqia can feel a wide gulf opening between them, one she can't hope to reach across. Not anymore.

Suddenly everything feels swimmy. She puts her hand out to the bedpost to steady herself. "I didn't want you to have to leave. But Eddie—"

"*Aarggh!* I *hate* him."

"Fine, but don't be mad at *me!*"

Anabelle turns around and stares at Raqia with revulsion, like some awful thing she's never seen before. Raqia looks down to find the bruises, actually there, slowly darkening. She can't feel them at all. They're blooming onto her skin beneath the hem of her skirt, she sees them when she peeks inside her T-shirt. Real. They're *real*. Her first impulse is to panic; she starts sweating.

"Eddie!" Anabelle shrieks. She jumps up and Chuy leaps away from her. "Get in here!" Anabelle looks like she wants to put out her hand toward Raqia but then stops. She folds her arms up tight and refuses to come any closer. "I can't believe you," she says to her, her voice both scared and furious.

Eddie comes in quickly, just as Raqia feels like she's falling, and steadies her. "Yeah, I thought so," he says, helping her to sit on the edge of Anabelle's bed. "Hang on, Rocky, you're going to be okay."

She looks up at him through a fog. He keeps telling her that, but how can he know?

"Shh, don't worry," he says and pulls up his sleeve. There, on his skin, are the same blue-gray mandalas that are appearing on hers.

She wants to scream but her voice comes out in a squeak. "How have I never seen those before? Why do I have them?"

"This is—it's just—terrible," Anabelle says, trepidation halting her voice. Suddenly she digs Chuy out from under her bed and clings to him. "It means you're a wolf, too."

"*What?*" Raqia shrieks. "A wolf? But I—I'm not—I can't—" Her throat is raw and she can barely form her thoughts into coherent—

Wait. She has—this is an *affinity*. She has an affinity, and suddenly all the doors in the world are yawning open to her, and behind them, mysterious darkness and incomprehensible—

She hears herself laughing in shock, maniacal, giddy, terrified. Her voice clamps in a shriek.

"What do I do now?" she half whispers, beseeching Anabelle, reaching out her hand. "I can't believe it."

But her best friend only grunts, then she says, "Don't be an idiot, on top of everything else."

"Hey, just because you're still Plain doesn't give you the right to be pissed at her," Eddie snaps. "No one chooses this, or when it happens." He turns to Raqia and gestures toward their mandalas. "The tattoos aren't common. They've only started happening recently, in our generation, and not very often. We don't know why yet." He shrugs, a little helplessly. "They only appear the first time, and then...when other new wolves are around. Mine turned up again last night—I saw them after I took you home." How is it he looks sheepish now? "And then I convinced myself it must have been because of the fight. One of the guys must be—" He sighs. "This is flimsy." Then he looks back at her eyes. "I'm sorry, I should have called to warn you, but I didn't want to wake you up."

Raqia is confused, drowning, mentally gasping for something to start making sense. "And what about—what about the sickness?" Her voice feels like she's pushing it through a strainer. "Did you feel that too? Is it normal to get so sick when your affinity emerges?" She hasn't heard about that before, but maybe—

Eddie shakes his head slowly, wiping away a hopefulness Raqia didn't realize she's been feeling.

"It's not normal at all," Anabelle says, judgment seeping through. "Affinities aren't a sickness." She sniffs. "Well, *good* ones aren't." Anabelle clutches her cat tighter until it hisses and swipes at her face and jumps out of her arms. She touches the scratch on her cheek as the cat flees, and her eyes fill with tears. "Get out of my room," she says, her voice low and hurt, "both of you."

Eddie helps Raqia to her feet—she feels steadier now—and pulls her by the hand to leave. "There's no talking sense to her," he says.

"*No,*" Raqia says, snatching her hand away from him. "You tell me now what your problem is, Anabelle."

"Today? It's *you.*"

Raqia's brain feels numb though her skin tingles. A fever is on her, she really is burning from the inside. She stares at the mandalas all over her body, growing ever more pronounced, larger, bleeding into each other. Then fine, soft hairs sprout from them, downy fur covering her skin, itching under her clothes. She touches her face gingerly; the "peach fuzz" she's always had is growing thicker, longer. Her fingernails seem longer, too. More shapely. Fierce.

Anabelle keeps staring at her. Eddie is tensed, ready to pounce if needed. Raqia can hear both their heartbeats.

"I don't think we can be friends anymore," Anabelle says. Her lip is shaking, her eyes filling up. "Wolves are dangerous." She glares pointedly at Eddie even as her tears start to fall. "They take things that don't belong to them. They hurt people."

What has Eddie taken from her? But then Raqia realizes it doesn't matter. Anabelle is Plain and jealous and doesn't care. Maybe it's time *she* doesn't care, either.

Suddenly filled with rage, Raqia runs from the room, runs past Eddie, who follows her, runs down the stairs. Anabelle slams her bedroom door behind them, crying loudly now. Ears ringing and her vision cloudy, Raqia nearly trips over Chuy hiding in the curve of the bottom step.

That cat is never going to help Anabelle find herself. Raqia can hear the rhythmic thump of its heart, can smell its bones and blood and tendons, can almost taste the dander of its fur in the air. That cat will never be what Anabelle wants, no matter how much she tries to make it so.

Feeling feral, unstoppable, Raqia scoops the animal up and crushes it in a vicious embrace. The thing hisses as it jerks away from her, lets out a long, angry screech and scratches at Raqia's chin, but she squeezes it, growling in her chest—a sound that terrifies her with its vibration and timbre—as if crushing the cat can drain her fury and fear.

Then suddenly amidst the howling and hissing and unmooring power in Raqia's hands there is Eddie. He's pulling Raqia's arms open, shoving Chuy out of the way. The cat escapes in a frenzy of claws and torn fur and scratchy yowls and then Raqia's arms are crushing Eddie, and she's screaming.

"Shh, Rocky, you're okay, you're safe."

She can hear his voice, but how, *how* can he be right? She wants to shred and bite and wreck—is this a Big Bad instinct? Is that what's making her feel sick? Every cell in her body screeches and howls at the overwhelming confusion of mind and body, of lurid thought and destructive impulse. His heartbeat is pounding in her ears, she can smell him, there, underneath the cedarwood and clean soap scent, it's him, his skin, his blood, it's overwhelming. She begins to flail her arms.

Eddie holds her elbows firmly to her sides, keeping her from moving until she looks into his face. He's blurry, his dark eyes intense and wavering at the same time; her cheeks feel wet and she realizes she's sobbing. It takes a minute, but gradually she stills herself, trying to even out her breaths, trying to keep the noise in.

Eddie smiles. "There we go." He puts one strong hand on her shoulder, and the other soothes away her tears. "Trust me, killing a small animal isn't the way you want to start this off."

She knows instinctively this both is and isn't a joke. In spite of the maelstrom inside her, she laughs, a choking sound spinning the violence down, her fear being strangled by the absurd.

"Besides, we don't want Anabelle to think her god-cat is only mortal, do we?" He's still smiling softly, smoothing her hair and her fury at the same time.

Raqia feels her gut clench and wants to vomit. Her throat is dry, burning. She rasps, "It was—an accident." Wasn't it? She can't actually kill something. Can she? But she wasn't able to stop herself. She looks up the stairs at the door to Anabelle's bedroom, can hear its slam resounding in her head, can hear Anabelle crying through the door. She looks at Eddie again, his dark eyes infinite as mystery. How does he manage all of this? Is it the same for him? What keeps him from *turning?*

Eddie puts his arm around her shoulders. "Come on, I'll take you home."

What will Taita think? What will she *do*? Her grandmother has given up everything, everything but Raqia, to protect her. How can she face her? Raqia feels the soft hair that has sprung out of her, that already feels thinner, finer than it did in Anabelle's bedroom, and the nausea she felt last night starts to bubble back up.

"Don't worry, I'll talk to her with you."

Taita likes Eddie, probably even loves him, but as she so resolutely pointed out, he isn't family.

Raqia wants to hide herself. "Do you have a hoodie I can wear?"

He touches her cheek lightly with the backs of his fingers and she shivers. "You don't need one," he says. "This'll go away soon." He nods his head toward the front door. "Come on." He smiles down at her. "Trust me."

She swallows hard and takes slow, deep breaths until the nausea subsides. She lets him lead her out of the house and down the driveway, but the whole time she keeps trying to find herself in what she's just done to Anabelle's cat. Was that her? She can't understand—what *is* she now?

And Eddie—she stops and looks at him. Something in his gaze both comforts and unsettles her.

"Everything's going to be fine, I promise."

She thinks about Anabelle and feels another wave of sick. The balance of—what is left of—their trio has shifted forever, but she can't tell whether Eddie is oblivious to this fact or triumphant in it. He pulls her along.

She takes a deep breath. She isn't Plain. She has an affinity and...power. She can feel it vibrating inside of her, singing in her blood. She thinks of the way people react to Eddie; what will they say about *her*—what will they think now? Will she feel like she belongs—belongs to what? She startles herself by imagining her newly sharp fingernails shredding that bully Alain's coxcomb right off his head.

She stops short and Eddie halts. "What is it?"

"I need to talk to Anabelle." This is not the way she wants their friendship to end. She doesn't want it to end at all.

He shakes his head. "I don't think that's wise right now."

"But—"

"Later. Give yourself time." He glances back up at the house to Anabelle's window. "Give her time, too." He looks into Raqia's eyes then. His own are dark and fiery and swallowing all at the same time. "Now let's get you home."

She stands very still until every dizzy, swimmy feeling has passed. Taita will have to understand. Then she remembers what Taita said: *I don't know, habibti... These wolves today are not like the wolves I knew... Back then, a wolf and a lamb could still be friends.*

Raqia doesn't want to believe she has Big Bad tendencies. She can show Taita that things will be all right, that wolves are more than what people see on television—although she'll need Eddie's help for that. She can still make Taita proud of her, surely. There *has* to be a way.

She hopes she isn't being naïve.

A grotesque montage of the past weeks' news bulletins flashes through her mind at that moment, but she squelches them hard until everything inside of her is quiet, still, dark. She can study them later.

Actually, yes. Yes, she *can*. Nothing can keep her out of an Affinities Studies program now. She can study anything she wants.

But not right now, she thinks. *One thing at a time.*

As she and Eddie travel across the street together, she traces the mandalas on her forearm beneath the fur growing out of them and shivers, filled with terror and delight.

12

W HEN THEY GET TO the front door, Eddie just stands there, waiting for Raqia to open it. Not forcing her to confront anything, least of all Taita, before she's ready to. Surprisingly, Raqia can hear the vacuum cleaner running on the other side of the house.

"Are my senses going to be heightened now?" she asks.

Eddie seems to know what she means. He shrugs. "Probably some, yes. Your hearing and vision, especially at night, will probably be sharper. You'll be a little stronger, a little faster than you were before."

Okay, so those changes will be nice. "And my emotions?"

Eddie sighs. "It takes a determined will to keep them in check, especially for the first few years."

That tracks with what she remembers of Eddie's middle school experience. "And after that?"

He tilts his head, his expression serious. "I'm not that much older than you, Rocky."

And he still struggles at times to keep on an even keel. Not often—Eddie is unusually strict with himself. But she remembers dancing with him last night, and the way his fingers tightened on her waist. The sharp edge in his eyes, his voice when the fight broke out. Why she felt the need to restrain him, to put a hand on his chest to prevent him from joining the fray. The way she wants to touch him now.

"So you're saying it's still difficult sometimes," she concludes.

"Sometimes," he whispers, his gaze intense.

The vacuum cleaner's shrill hum winds down, and Raqia's breath catches in her throat. She stares at her front door.

"Are you ready to go in yet?" Eddie murmurs.

Her hand gets as far as touching the doorknob, but she can't make it turn. She just can't do it yet. She shakes her head rapidly.

Eddie exhales quietly and glances at his phone, returns it to the back pocket of his jeans.

"Did you finish packing?" she asks, quietly so Taita won't hear them.

"Mostly." He shrugs. "Don't worry about it. I have time." He leads her away from the door, off the tiny front porch, back down the driveway. "Let's go to the park for a little while."

She touches the fur vanishing from her skin. Even the mandalas are starting to fade. Maybe they can stay at the park just until she looks normal again.

Normal. This is her new normal. She has an affinity. *This is normal.* Well, mostly. They still don't know why she got so sick. Or why the mandalas have started appearing when wolves emerge.

And, oh no—she tried to crush Anabelle's cat out of rage and fear. That was not normal. There's a chasm, Raqia realizes, between what "normal" is and the details she's going to need to parse out about what's happening to her. Probably.

"You're being very quiet," Eddie says. "How're you feeling?" They've made it down the block and froggered their way across a busy street. One more block and they'll be right by the elementary school and its attached park.

"I'm...not nauseated anymore," she tells him.

"Good."

"And I don't feel feverish now, either."

He nods his head, smiles. They seem to be moving quickly down the sidewalk. A comfortable pace, but faster than she usually walks with Anabelle. Eddie is a head taller than she is, his legs longer than hers, but she's keeping up with him without any trouble. When they get to the corner of the school grounds, she glances down at her arms. The fur is all but gone, the mandalas no darker than two-week-old henna.

"Let's hit the swings," Eddie suggests, opening the chain-link gate at the edge of the park. Not many people are out, other than a few kids playing basketball on the far end.

They each take a swing, wrap their hands around the heavy chains holding the seats to the tall metal structure. Raqia loved the swingset when she was growing up, could ride it for hours if Taita would let her. She has a strong urge to push herself into the air now, swing a deep arc and ride it as high as she can go, and then jump into the air like a bird.

But she is not a bird.

Eddie calmly sways back and forth, his sneakers anchoring him to the dirt below their feet. She mimics his movement.

"You must have questions," he finally says.

"I don't even know where to start."

"That's fair. It's overwhelming in the beginning."

"Do you think I would have really killed Chuy?"

He smirks. "Nope." Pops the "p" sound.

"It felt like I was going to." She swallows hard. "It felt like I *wanted* to."

He levels his gaze at her. "No way I'd have let you."

"But you aren't going to be here all the time. I have to be able to control this on my own."

He nods. He can't deny it.

"And what about Anabelle? How long is she going to stay mad at me?" She adds under her breath, "Stupidly mad. This isn't my fault."

"Listen, Rocky, because this is important. There is no *fault* here. Affinities are not some...I don't know, *moral* question. You have one or you don't. No one chooses what they are. Taita gets owl. My dad gets bear, my mom gets gazelle. You—and I—get wolf. We don't know yet what Anabelle will get, or when, or if. There's nothing anyone can do to slow down or speed up this process. We get no say."

An edge to his tone betrays a sense of helplessness. Raqia breathes a silent gratitude that she isn't in seventh grade when this is happening to her.

She chooses her words carefully. "And Anabelle's likely to be upset because I suddenly got an affinity at the same time she was losing out."

"Losing out?"

"With Taylor, the boy she likes." She reaches out to flick his shoulder. "Pay attention, Eddie."

He grabs her hand and holds it close to his heart. "I am. You suddenly have more than one thing she doesn't."

She takes a couple of deep breaths to slow down her racing pulse. Forces herself to stay on the swing. When she slowly withdraws her hand he doesn't stop her, but he also doesn't break eye contact with her.

She turns away first, looks toward the sky. The sun has begun its languid descent. How many hours till sundown and she has to go home? Not many, this late in the year.

She pushes her legs back and forth to start the swing. Not too high. "Did you know any other wolves when you got your affinity?"

He checks the time on his phone again, sighs almost imperceptibly—but she hears it. Then he mirrors her movement, also not going too high. "I did not."

"How did you learn how to..."

He grins. "Be a wolf?"

"Yeah."

"Trial and error? Boy scout camping trips?" He laughs. "It's not like I—" He shakes his head, slows his swing back down. He puts a hand out toward her, gently, until she slows down, too. "Look, we don't turn into beasts and run through the woods howling at the full moon. Affinities aren't like that."

She knows this, intellectually, of course. Hadn't she just reminded Anabelle that Taita couldn't fly? But everything in her head feels jumbled. Wolves are different; everyone keeps saying so. *Aggressive, dangerous.* The feverish feeling begins again, heating her from the inside. She stares down at her skin. The mandalas have faded even more, only vague outlines still visible. The fur is all gone. But she doesn't feel *normal*. She wants to run and shriek and crush, her entire body vibrating. She starts the swing again, this time pumping her legs hard to arc up as high as she can.

"Rocky, please slow down. We need to talk about things before I leave."

She jumps off the swing, lands easily on the grass ten feet away. A ripple of calm washes over her, replaced almost immediately with that burning sensation again.

"I can't do this, Eddie," she says, her voice straining with panic. "I'm all over the place right now. It feels like the fever is back. I can't go home like this." And she can't go to Anabelle's. How is she going to manage this? Is she also actually sick on top of everything else? Or is this just anxiety? "And you have to go back to school."

He walks toward her, puts his arms around her, holding the panic in. "You *can* do this. When it feels like you're going to spiral out, explode, just take some deep breaths. Imagine everything spinning down small. It takes practice."

His voice is quiet, soothing. She clings back, feeling the fear disperse as if he has absorbed it all away. If only she could burrow into this moment, freeze it in time.

"And I won't be gone long," he says. "Not now."

She hates herself for asking, doesn't want to be part of his decision, but she says, "You're going to transfer?"

"I already told you I was." He clears his throat, a low rumble she can feel. "I started the process three weeks ago. I'll be enrolling at either Rice or U of H by January."

She looks up sharply. "I thought you were only considering it."

He shrugs, but his gaze on her is steady. Somehow it makes her feel better, and she isn't sure she wants that.

"And I'll be back in town again next weekend. Our team is playing here on Saturday."

She almost laughs. Why didn't she ever expect that to happen? "Is your dad going to make us all come watch you play?"

He grins, a mischievous glint in his eye. He knew how much Anabelle hated doing that in high school. "What, you don't want to?"

A fierce wave fills her up again. She tightens her hands around his arms, then before she can even think about it, reaches up and kisses him, hard. On the lips. Then immediately rushes back away from him, the air between their bodies stretching thin into a vacuum.

"I'm sorry! I didn't mean—"

But she *did*. She did.

Eddie stands eerily still. Watching her. A guarded look on his face, and his hands slowly clenching at his sides. Releasing. A deep, quiet breath.

"Don't say you didn't mean it," he murmurs.

She just nods her head, afraid to take even a single step closer to him. The breeze picks up, maybe the first one in months that isn't just a hot wind, and she can hear every airy whisper through the leaves of the park's trees. It's getting later.

"You have to go back to school," she whispers, her throat suddenly dry.

He shrugs, otherwise not moving.

"Are you...are you mad at me? I shouldn't have—"

"Not even a little bit." His most subtle smile peeks out. "If I come closer to you, are you going to run off or hit me or anything?"

She can't say what she'll do, so she says nothing. He takes a step forward. She doesn't move. Another step. Soon he's standing right there, just a few inches away. He takes both her hands in his, anchors her to the ground with his touch. All the fight and panic leave her.

"I'm scared," she whispers.

"I know. But are you scared of me?"

She shakes her head.

He smiles. "Good." Gently holds her face in his hands. Leans over and kisses her. Lingers there. His kiss is quiet, soft, nothing wolfish about it at all.

And that, more than anything he has said, makes her imagine a world where she can be a wolf and *not* be out of control. She can be calm. She puts her arms around him, relaxes into this quiet moment.

He breaks away and leans his forehead to hers. "Feeling better?"

"Much," she admits.

"Good. But I didn't do that just to settle you down."

It's her turn to smile. "I know."

"Is that okay? Things are going to change."

Anabelle is already mad at her. Raqia will have to work things out with her, somehow. She doesn't see how an...evolving relationship with Eddie can make that much worse. So she nods. "It's okay."

He kisses her again, then runs his hands slowly up and down her arms. The mandalas are entirely gone now, too. "It's late. Let me take you back home."

"Right. But I'm not ready to tell Taita yet. About any of this."

"I know. But you can't wait forever."

"Can it wait until you come back?" She wants him to be there. Somehow that seems like it might be easier. A small part of her feels guilty about that, but...one emotion at a time.

He shrugs. "Maybe. Five days is a long time to hide something like this."

They walk back, their shadows lengthening. They hold hands all the way to her house.

"You're going to be late getting back to school," she says. "I'm sorry."

"I'm not." He smiles. "I'll call you when I get there."

"That sounds great." Does she hug him good-bye? Kiss him? If Taita or Anabelle were to look outside, they would see.

He glances back across to his house, maybe thinking the same thing. Then turns back to her and kisses her slowly, his lips teasing hers apart. Breaks away first. "See you soon."

She can't help but smile back as he crosses the street. Waves at her from his front door, goes inside the house.

Somehow, she has to do the same.

She takes a deep breath, then walks up to her front door, turns the knob, and manages to smile at her grandmother, who's doing a crossword puzzle at the kitchen table.

"Feeling better?" Taita asks warmly as she moves her reading glasses down her beaky nose, the better to see Raqia as she walks in.

"I am." And that's not a lie, no matter how jumbled up things are inside. Raqia kisses her cheek and then sits down at the table across from her. Suddenly, her stomach rumbles. "What's for dinner?"

Taita laughs softly. "Whatever your stomach can tolerate."

"My appetite is definitely back." Raqia stretches. "But I'm pretty tired. I might turn in early." The less time she spends around Taita, the less likely she'll blurt out her new developments, ones she doesn't yet have the language for to express to her grandmother in any way that will seem safe to her.

"That makes sense," Taita says. "You need your rest, habibti, as much as you can get after you have been ill."

She puts her crossword puzzle book away and begins moving around the kitchen, taking dishes out of the refrigerator and a few fresh vegetables. She puts a small bowl of hummus and a loaf of pita on the table in front of Raqia, who digs into it eagerly.

"Do you not want to wait until I have put the olive oil on it?" Taita asks. "No paprika?"

Raqia gives her a closed-mouth grin, cheeks full of bread and hummus. "No need."

She's about the dip the bread back into the bowl when her phone buzzes from the pocket of her skirt. It's a text from Eddie.

I'm leaving for school now. He tells her again, **I'll call when I get there**

Raqia smiles and likes his message, then puts her phone down just as it buzzes again. Another text from him.

I already miss you

She imagines him grinning at his phone in the dark of the car while his dad drives him back to school. How his dark hair has probably fallen into his eyes. How his dad is probably talking to him about football, and how Eddie is probably not listening to him.

She hovers a moment before liking this second text, but she does it.

So it looks like they're doing this. *Okay.* She takes another bite, famished. *It'll be okay.*

She hopes.

13

MONDAY MORNING COMES AROUND with a pounding headache and that feverish feeling again. Nausea has also re-entered the scene. Raqia wakes up and vomits all of last night's dinner, then lies down on the cold bathroom floor. She can feel her own pallor and worries whether this sickness is related to her affinity's emergence, her fear that her grandmother will find out about it, or something else entirely.

This is how Taita finds her. She tells Raqia to get back into bed.

"You are not going to school in this condition," she clucks and fusses, pulling the blankets up to Raqia's chin and feeling her forehead for a temperature. "I am calling your doctor as soon as their office opens."

Raqia nods and sinks farther into her pillow. Taita's right, but what will Anabelle think about her absence? She reaches for her phone and sees Eddie's last text from the night before, wishing her sweet dreams. It makes her smile. They stayed on the phone last night for a couple of hours after he got back to school. They talked some about his own transition in seventh grade, but mostly about what college was like and what he was hoping to do when he got back home and transferred. Even though he talked more about engineering and how much he missed living in a big city, two undercurrents leaked out now and then.

He wanted to stay closer to his friends still in high school, since some of them had already shown wolf affinities and he wanted to be a good influence; he didn't say it outright, but it seemed he wanted to balance out Luke's charismatically hostile tendencies.

"Anabelle and I call him Puppyface," Raqia said.

Eddie laughed, the sound smooth and rich like dark chocolate. "He must love that."

"Well, I didn't know his name yet. You do realize that Anabelle can't stand him."

"I got that impression." He was quiet a second before asking, "I'm curious what you think of him—other than choosing possibly the most condescending nickname imaginable."

Raqia thought carefully before answering. "He's an instigator. He says things just to upset us." She considered how quickly he jumped into the fight at the dance. "And he looks like he might be violent, given any opportunity."

Eddie made a sound of grudging assent. "Maybe I can steer him away from that. It's part of why I'm coming back home for good in November." His college was on the quarter system, so his term ended before Thanksgiving. "I want to do something that will make a positive difference in the world." His voice took on a slightly teasing tone. "Starting with turning an obnoxious teenage boy into a decent man might be a good start."

Raqia laughed. "Good luck."

Also, though he didn't say it in so many words, he clearly missed being part of a trio with Raqia and Anabelle. And if she listened carefully to what he stopped himself from saying, she could tell he missed *her*. A small spot of warmth glowed inside of her at that. Eddie's feelings seemed both sudden and, somehow, a natural extension of their friendship.

This morning, she considers the speed at which they have gone from being childhood friends and neighbors to...is this *dating*? Is it a relationship? Maybe it will become clearer when she sees him again this weekend.

What will Anabelle think? What will she do? Raqia sighs and texts her: **sick again. Taita won't let me come to school, probably a doctor visit in my immediate future.** She hesitates only a moment before typing: **call me when you get home?**

It's already 8:30 in the morning. Anabelle will be on her way to history class by now.

Three little dots finally show up, bouncing slowly on the side of the screen. Disappear. Bounce again. Disappear again. Then nothing for a long minute.

Finally a tiny thumbs-up emoji appears in response to Raqia's last text. Anabelle is probably still mad but probably also willing to at least talk to her. Maybe they can work this out after school. Hopefully so—Raqia doesn't want to lose her friendship. Besides the fact that her social circle is embarrassingly small, she and Anabelle have built their bond over years. It seems like such a waste to lose that in a weekend.

She considers texting Eddie, too, to let him know she's sick again. He would want to know. But she doesn't want him to worry; she's doing enough of that for both of them. Better to wait until she sees her doctor anyway, so then she'll have something useful to tell him. It feels a little strange having someone besides just Taita and Anabelle to care about how she's doing. Strange, but nice, too.

Suddenly a chill comes over her whole body, shaking it under the blankets. She burrows down farther, curls herself into a ball. A wave of fatigue washes over her. Maybe if she can just close her eyes for a while...

She must fall asleep because the next thing she knows, Taita is gently shaking her awake.

"Come, habibti, I am taking you to the doctor. You have an appointment at eleven."

Raqia blinks a few times. The light coming from her window is brighter, less slanted. The whole room feels warm. She pushes the blankets back, stretches. Her eyes grow clear quickly.

"What time is it now?"

Taita feels Raqia's forehead again and says, "Ten-fifteen. We must leave in twenty minutes." She moves around the room, gathering a T-shirt and lounge pants from Raqia's dresser.

Raqia quickly peeks inside her long-sleeve pajama top to see if the mandalas have come back. They haven't, at least not on her chest or stomach or arms.

"It's okay, I can do it," she tells Taita, who has returned with fresh clothes. "I'll be ready soon. I can do it."

Taita nods. "Do not fall back asleep, habibti," she cautions.

"I won't," Raqia says as her grandmother leaves the room and closes the door behind her.

While she rinses off quickly in the shower and gets ready to leave, Raqia inspects her body for any changes at all—mandalas, fur, claws—but sees nothing beyond her longer, more shapely fingernails. The polish looks two weeks old from the growth since she painted them—was it only three nights ago? Three days? The beginning of this past weekend feels astronomically distant now.

On the way to the doctor's office, Raqia emails her teachers to let them know she's sick and to ask them to let her know what her make-up work will be. She also sees a calendar invite for the next afternoon, a meeting with Anabelle and this guest speaker the Plain Isn't Pain club has brought in, scheduled for 3:30. Assuming she's feeling well enough to go to school, Raqia still plans to go, so she clicks *yes* on the invite to add it to her calendar. She just hopes Anabelle feels reassured by this Elsa woman's story.

At the office, the nurse ushers Raqia into an exam room, and Raqia is grateful that she's old enough not to have Taita there with her. She's still not ready to tell her about the wolf affinity landing on her after the dance. The nurse notes all the symptoms of Raqia's illness.

"One other thing," she says before the nurse leaves the room. "My...um, my animal affinity emerged this weekend."

The nurse smiles brightly. "Congratulations! What are you?"

Raqia mumbles more than speaks, "A wolf, I think."

"Ah." The nurse is still smiling with her mouth but not her eyes. "Have you told anyone yet?"

"Not my grandmother," Raqia says.

The nurse nods knowingly. "Well, be sure to bring it up with the doctor." Then she leaves, and Raqia shivers slightly as the air conditioning shifts quietly on.

A few minutes later, when the doctor clops in, he takes one look at Raqia and says, "Hey, kiddo. You seem to have had a rough weekend."

"Yeah."

He scratches his long, narrow face while he looks at her chart and ticks off each symptom, then shrugs. "You don't have a temperature now. How are you feeling?"

"Okay, I guess." Other than a slight case of existential dread, that is. "My nausea is gone again, and I'm feeling better rested after my nap this morning."

"Yup." He inspects her eyes and ears and nose and throat. He listens to her chest and back with a stethoscope. She lies down on the exam bench, and he presses gently on each side of her abdomen with blocky hands. "Any pain here?"

"Nope."

"That's good. You can sit up now."

She does, and he sits on the rolling stool to talk to her. "What all did you eat this weekend?"

She lists everything from the giant bowl of pasta Friday night to the small loaf of warmed pita this morning.

"And do you feel sick when you think about any of those?"

"The pasta, a little bit. I don't think I want to order it again."

"And are you hungry now?"

She hadn't considered it until he asked. "I am, actually. I kind of want some more pita, with butter this time." Her stomach rumbles. "And maybe also a cheeseburger."

The doctor smiles. "Well, try the bread first, and if that goes well, maybe get a small-size cheeseburger and see how you feel after that. And then if nothing else causes you any trouble, I'm going to chalk this up to a mild case of food poisoning or maybe just a twenty-four-hour stomach bug."

Raqia nods. It's a small relief. "There's one more thing, though."

"I'm listening."

"Is it normal for people to get sick like this when their animal affinity comes out?"

The doctor shakes his head. "That doesn't normally happen. Why?"

"I haven't told my grandmother about this yet, but I think I got mine this weekend. Yesterday, in fact."

"That's good news! Why don't you want to tell her yet?"

"It's...complicated. I don't think she'll approve."

He shakes his head again to flick his longish black hair back over his shoulder and says, not unkindly, "It's not like it's something you can choose, Raqia."

"I know, but...this one is bad. I mean, maybe."

"Do you feel like you're bad because of it?"

"No! But I'm worried about what she'll think of me."

The doctor sighs quietly. "I don't think it's a good idea to try to hide this from her. Were you not at home when the transformation came on you?"

Raqia shakes her head. "I was at a friend's house." She tells him about the fur and the mandalas and how they disappeared after a couple of hours, and how Eddie's mandalas came on him again, too.

"Mandalas?" he asks. "Do you still have them?"

She shakes her head. "They're completely gone. I took a picture of them, though." She pulls out her phone and shows him a couple of images she took of the designs on her arms, after Eddie had calmed her down enough not to freak out about them.

"Interesting," the doctor says. "I haven't seen them in person before, my-self, but I've read about them. Not all wolves get them, but they're becoming more common."

"Do you think I need to be worried?"

"No evidence suggests anything about them is dangerous."

"But wolves *are*."

"They *can* be. But it's not a given; you know that."

She nods, thinking of Eddie. She *does* know that.

After regarding her thoughtfully a moment longer, the doctor says, "Look, you're still a minor. That means your grandmother has access to your medical records, and your affinity is going to be marked in there. I don't have to tell her myself, because she has legal access to the information if she looks into your chart online."

Raqia knows this intellectually but begins to feel a little panicked thinking about Taita discovering on her own that she's gotten her affinity. What if she looks it up while Raqia is at school? Her pulse starts to race and she puts a hand to her heart.

"How are you feeling now?" the doctor asks. "You're looking pale. Do you feel nauseated again?"

It's not nausea this time. The illness that brought her here doesn't seem to be coming back. And she still kind of wants a cheeseburger, so this must be something else. Raqia shakes her head. "Just anxious, I think."

"Getting your affinity is a good thing."

"I know." She sits still for a bit longer, till she feels calm again, while the doctor observes. He doesn't seem concerned and that makes Raqia feel a little better.

"I can't promise you how things will turn out," he finally says, "but I do think it's clear that affinities don't really alter our personalities that much. Not on a fundamental level."

She has heard this before, but it helps a little to hear it from a medical professional.

"Think about all of your friends who have their affinities."

She doesn't tell him how very short a list that is.

She wishes Anabelle had gotten hers over the weekend, too, so they could be going through this together. So Anabelle wouldn't feel so angry.

"Did any of them change on a deep level when their affinities emerged? Or were they the same, just enhanced, more mature." That last part isn't really a question.

She thinks about Eddie, and about a couple of the other girls she used to know well back in middle school, before their affinities emerged. And the doctor is right: their personalities didn't really change, not in any lasting way, once the flush of transformation had passed.

"I guess not," she answers.

"So why would yours?"

She doesn't have a satisfying response to this, no answer that could justify her worries, so she just shrugs.

"I get the sense that there's something else going on here, Raqia." His voice is calming, reassuring. "Do you want to talk about it a little more?"

"It's just...wolves aren't great. I mean, some wolves. Obviously."

"I know the news is scary right now. But let's think about this another way. Do you know any wolves personally?"

She nods.

"And what are they like?"

She takes a deep breath. Eddie is aggressive on the football field, but in real life he's good-hearted, smart, fun to be around. It seems like her feelings for him are evolving as fast as her own physiology. And maybe like her previously latent affinity, they were inevitable after years of playing together and teasing and growing up side by side. That familiarity is intense.

But then his friends... She doesn't have a good read on any of them but Puppyface.

"They're okay," she says. "I mean, mostly. I have a close friend who's definitely not a Big Bad, and he has a friend who might be. But Taita is not going to like this."

"Why do you assume that? Does she not like your close friend?"

"It's not that." Her doctor doesn't know about their family's history before they emigrated. "My mother was killed by someone with a wolf affinity, back in Lebanon, when I was a toddler."

The doctor exhales heavily, slowly nods his head. "I can see why you're feeling anxious about it."

"She wasn't targeted or anything—at least, I don't think she was. She was just swept up in a series of attacks, in the wrong place at the wrong time." So many people were.

The doctor gently checks her pulse and listens to her breathing one more time. "Raqia, I think you may be suffering from generalized anxiety, most likely about your affinity and your family's tragic association with wolves in the past."

She was beginning to form that same conclusion. Raqia's mother was just one more statistical data point. And if she could wrap her head around the data, understand what led to those statistics in the first place, she might be able to resolve some of her feelings about it.

She says, "I've been thinking about going into Affinity Behavioralism as a field."

He smiles. "That sounds like a great idea. Very proactive of you." He rolls his chair back to the cabinets on the wall and takes out a brochure. "You know about the research study coming out of A&M, right?" Hands it to her. Dr. Delacoeur's face is on the cover, with the name of the study and her contact information. "If you read that, you'll see the scope of the project. They're looking for interns this summer."

"But I don't want to be studied myself," she says. "Won't she try to recruit me if I'm a wolf?"

"Not necessarily. Participation as a subject is strictly voluntary. And the research interns can have any affinity—or even none at all. Your perspective, as a young wolf, could be valuable."

And studying the problem might help her understand it better, make her less anxious about it. "I'll consider it," she says and folds up the brochure to stuff into her pocket. "Thank you."

He nods. "And like I said before, I don't need to tell your grandmother anything." He gives her a reassuring smile. "But you probably do. You know what I mean?"

Raqia nods, because she does. And she can't wait forever.

But if she can wait just until Eddie gets back this weekend, so he can be there, too... Somehow that idea makes her feel better, makes the conversation feel more manageable. If she tells Taita she's not sick anymore and can go back to school tomorrow, then hopefully Taita won't feel any need to look up Raqia's medical chart online.

She just has to make it through a few more days.

14

ON TUESDAY RAQIA FEELS well enough to go to school. In fact, her symptoms from the food poisoning—she's going to assume, in the absence of other information, that this is what was making her physically sick Saturday night—have gone, and even her anxiety has subsided. Her first chance to see Anabelle—who texted her the day before to say she had a ton of homework and couldn't talk—is in assembly, when the guest speaker the Plain Isn't Pain club has brought in will speak to the whole school. Raqia goes to their usual spot on the left side of the auditorium; they always get seats on the aisle near the back so they can get out quickly after assembly ends. But when she gets there, Anabelle hasn't saved Raqia's seat; instead, she's sitting with a couple of other girls from her English class.

"Hey," Raqia says in greeting, feeling uncertain. All three girls look up at her.

"Hey," Anabelle says back. And then looks at Raqia with impassive eyes and a thin line for a mouth. The other two girls look at them both and then continue their conversation on either side of Anabelle.

"So, how are you?" Raqia asks.

Anabelle shrugs. "Fine." A pause. "Are you still sick?"

"No. My doctor said it was food poisoning."

"Cool." Anabelle shrugs. "See you later."

That cuts.

So now what? Raqia looks around to scout any other empty seats nearby; the aisle chairs have filled up quickly, so no matter where she goes, she'll be scooting past someone's legs to sit down, which is awkward at best and opens her up to snide comments at worst.

Except...she isn't Plain anymore. The low growl building in her chest at Anabelle's coldness reminds Raqia that she can sit anywhere she wants to and no one can say anything about it—

But how will people know her affinity has come? The physical transformation lasted only a few hours. Not very long, but not unusually short, either.

She scans the nearby rows again and sees Kirstin from the homecoming group with an empty seat next to her several rows up. *Leopard print ribbon girl,* Raqia thinks, remembering her mum, and wonders whether she ended up tripping over it that night. Before she can even think twice, Raqia has walked over and is standing next to Kirstin's row.

"Um, hi." The girl looks up at Raqia, her long black fingernails slowly drumming on the arm of her chair. "Can I sit next to you?"

Kirstin looks Raqia over, narrows her dark eyes slightly, then nods. Raqia steps carefully past her and sits down just as the Plain Isn't Pain club president takes the microphone and begins talking. The rest of the student body grudgingly quiets down.

Kirstin tilts her head toward Raqia and whispers, "So. You and Eddie."

Raqia's hackles rise. *Me and Eddie what? You have an opinion?* "Yeah."

Kirstin smirks. "Interesting."

Of course, because she still thinks Raqia is Plain. She slacks the leash on that low growl just a little. A few of the people around them hear it and look at Raqia. She tries to keep eye contact with Kirstin as a tether for her nerves, which are threatening to explode.

Leopard print ribbon girl's eyes widen. Then she smiles, for real. "*Very* interesting," she whispers, then turns her attention back to the speaker, who has just come to the podium.

Raqia faces forward and focuses on the speaker too. Not only can she hear the muted whispers of some of the people around them, but she can also understand what they're saying—that's new. A comment about how dumb the Plain Isn't Pain club is; another comment about how different she, Raqia, seems today; a third comment about how stupid assemblies are. Raqia takes a deep, silent breath. Runs her longer fingernails across the pads of her thumbs. How many new things will she have to get used to in the coming days?

The speaker, who has introduced herself as Elsa, has a lot of curly blue-black hair piled up in a clip and a tailored, dark green suit on. She stands with the bearing of someone who has to remind herself she has confidence because she isn't used to it yet.

"I was Plain well into my thirties," she's saying. "In fact, I was so desperate to have an affinity I even tried to force my transformation." Her breath catches and she's quiet for a few seconds as she resets herself. "That was a grave mistake."

What did she try to do? That's not something you can—

"But I'm here to assure you that affinities *can* come later in life. So often we forget that those who are Plain can have a more challenging road ahead of them. My own circumstances were filled with...many hurdles, before my affinity emerged. And as you might expect, everything about my life situation changed when it became clear I had one. Of course, it didn't change who I am as a person."

The assembly grows restless, the dampered rustling of hundreds of teenage bodies shifting in their seats. She clears her throat and continues, a little more loudly.

"I had believed for most of my life that I had an allergy to water—certainly I had an aversion to it—and yet my affinity is an aquatic one. Sometimes I consider how much time I wasted in fear, in timidity. I knew, once my self finally emerged, that I had to take a more active role in the world. So over the past couple of years, since my transition, I've pursued a different, more fulfilling career track and now work with the Phoenix Group to provide outreach and counseling in many school districts, primarily at the high school level. We work with a wide variety..."

A low murmur spreads throughout the auditorium. Phoenix Group? Raqia hasn't heard of them before, but phoenixes are a taboo subject. Every once in a while a rumor of one appearing surfaces, but that's usually a hoax. Phoenixes are literally resurrected from the dead, sometimes after a miserable life as a Plain One, and they don't happen more than once in a generation—if at all. When did the last one even appear? In what country? Raqia has no idea if they're even real.

"Our organization works with the Plain community to achieve social justice. Equality in the working world, in housing, in all avenues of society." She presents a few slides with grim statistics about the struggles Plain Ones are experiencing, and it's a lot worse and a lot more widespread than Raqia realized. It goes far beyond school bullies like Alain. She feels an instinctive pit opening in her stomach that quells when she remembers this isn't her problem anymore. Then it yawns open again when she considers what Anabelle is probably feeling right now. As hurt as she is, Anabelle is still her best friend, and she cares about her. Surely this thing between them is just a rough patch.

Elsa continues speaking to the newly subdued auditorium full of teenagers. "I'll be conducting small group sessions throughout today and tomorrow, strictly voluntary, and there are still some timeslots available. You're welcome to make an appointment through the main office or with your guidance counselor, if you haven't already done so, and you can come by yourself or in a small group to learn more about what we do."

To learn more about what they do? That seems like a euphemistic cover story for anyone who wants therapy. Raqia guesses the Plain Isn't Pain club brought her in so that Plain students could feel better about themselves in the generally insensitive environment of adolescence, so they could feel reassured that their time would eventually come. Maybe that makes sense. As skeptical as she was, maybe last week Raqia might have found some value in it. Maybe Anabelle still will. And maybe the Phoenix Group can offer some suggestions about safely navigating the adult world as a Plain One. Raqia shudders.

After Elsa finishes speaking, there are a few more administrative announcements and reminders from the student body president about club meetings and an upcoming college application workshop. When the presentations are over, Raqia tries to catch Anabelle's eye as she stands up to leave, but her friend is engrossed in conversation with her new seatmates and barely waves at her as she leaves the auditorium. They'll see each other in class later, and for sure at the appointment with Elsa after school. Raqia has no need of Plainness counseling anymore, but she wants to be there for Anabelle. She still isn't sure what Elsa can do for her friend, but now she's curious to find out.

After the assembly, Raqia moves through her day with an internal vibration, a buzzing that raises the hair on her arms and the scruff of her neck every time someone comes too close. Her focus during classes feels like a tug-of-war between thoughts of Anabelle's arctic demeanor and the heated whispers she can hear quite clearly about the way she danced with Eddie on Saturday night. The possessive way he held her. She wonders if anyone saw her almost kiss him or if everyone was already distracted by the fight breaking out on the other side of the gym. So far no one has said anything directly to her. Raqia doesn't know what Kirstin might have said to anyone, or what she actually saw.

Halfway through math class, which Raqia and Anabelle have together, Raqia jots a note in her spiral and nudges it toward Anabelle. It reads, *lunch?*

Anabelle writes back, *don't you have to make up yesterday's biology quiz?*

Of course! Raqia forgot. She writes, *thanks—guess I'll see you later?*

Anabelle half shrugs and goes back to taking notes. They don't talk again after class, either, since their math teacher wants Raqia to stay behind to confirm what she missed yesterday, and during that conversation, Anabelle disappears.

As the clock reaches 3:30, Raqia arrives at the office to meet Anabelle for her appointment with the new counselor. When she taps Anabelle on the shoulder, her flinch surprises Raqia.

"What are you doing here?" Anabelle asks.

"I said I'd come with you." Why would she not expect Raqia to keep her promise?

"But it's not like you need it now."

Raqia never meant to come here for herself. How does Anabelle not realize that? "I'm here for you. Moral support, that sort of thing." Anabelle's sheepish side glance makes Raqia feel awkward. "What, did you not expect me to keep my promise? You wanted me here."

"Okay, okay." Anabelle ducks her head slightly, looks anxious. "Lower your voice."

"I wasn't shouting." Raqia's confused and more than a little insulted, but she matches Anabelle's stage whisper. "Just because I have my affinity now doesn't mean I'm going to abandon you. Honestly, what kind of friend would I be if I did that?"

Not a good one, and Anabelle's shifting eyes create a hollow feeling in Raqia's chest. Had their situations been reversed, had Anabelle gotten her affinity over the weekend instead, would she have dropped Raqia? The idea ices into the emptiness she feels.

The conference room door opens and the new counselor smiles brightly at them both. "Welcome!" she says, extending her hand to shake each of theirs. "You can call me Elsa. Come on in?"

They go in and sit on one side of the rectangular table, introduce themselves. Anabelle drops her backpack on the chair between them before Raqia can sit next to her. Rude, but whatever. Elsa closes the door and sits across from them, a pleasant smile on her face.

Anabelle begins, "I thought your story, the one you told in the assembly today, was interesting."

"Thank you." Elsa looks her in the eye while fiddling casually with a pen that has an iridescent scale pattern on it. "Although many people find their affinities during the teen years, I didn't discover mine until quite a bit later in life." She gestures to herself: a polished-looking, professional, grown adult. Maybe late thirties? It's hard to tell with Elsa's tastefully done make-up. "As you can see."

Raqia had been distracted by the murmurings of other students in the assembly, so clear to her newly sharpened sense of hearing, that she missed a lot of Elsa's origin story. Something about becoming a fish?

"What was it like, not having one for so long?" Anabelle is leaning forward so far in her chair she's practically resting on the edge of the conference table.

"I'm not going to lie," Elsa says. "It was hard. My parents and sister were embarrassed by my Plainness. It was hard to get a good job or a nice apartment."

"Yeah," Anabelle says quietly, as if she has any idea what that kind of life is really like.

"Were you always a counselor?" Raqia asks.

Elsa shakes her head, and her mass of dark hair threatens to fall right out of its clip. "No, I had an office job. My boss was...well, we used to call him the Monster Behind the Big Oak Desk." She half smiles. "When my affinity finally made itself known, the first thing I did was leave that company and find something else. Counseling seemed like a natural choice."

"Why?" Anabelle asks.

Elsa shrugs. "Because it was something I wish I'd had access to when I was younger." There's a pause while Anabelle, brow furrowed, seems to mull this over. "I had so much work experience and such a dogged work ethic that once my affinity emerged, I could have gone into any number of fields, but this seemed like a need that I could fill."

That's generous, kind. Therapy isn't a glamorous or stress-free kind of job.

"What kind of counseling do you do, for the most part?" Raqia asks.

"All kinds, related to animal affinities. For people who don't get theirs as early as they would like, for people who think they never will. And sometimes for people who aren't happy with the one they do get."

"Oh, well," Anabelle begins, the tiniest edge of sarcasm slithering into her voice as she casts a know-it-all look at Raqia. "That sounds useful, doesn't it?" She continues, to Elsa, "Raqia got her affinity this weekend."

Raqia is about to protest that she isn't unhappy about her affinity, but can she really say that? She doesn't know, honestly, how she feels about it yet. It's complicated. Anabelle's calling her out—which is what this feels like—isn't great, though.

Elsa glances between the two of them in the quiet that follows. Then she says quietly, "Congratulations." And then she asks Anabelle with a pointed look, "And how about you?"

"I don't have mine yet." Anabelle sniffs. "I was curious how...you said in the assembly that you tried to...I don't know, force it?"

Elsa shutters herself a little, seems more guarded. But her voice remains even and professional when she says, "I did. I had become so foolishly desperate that I began imagining signs all around me that I might ultimately become a phoenix."

Raqia shivers at that. Does this mean Elsa tried to...kill herself? How horrible. She sneaks a glance at Anabelle, whose face is more curious than appalled.

"I assume you aren't one, then?" Anabelle asks.

"No. And I'm extremely lucky to have lived to find that out. Affinities cannot be forced, no matter what you try."

Raqia considers Chuy, Anabelle's cat whom she almost crushed to death, and her friend's insistence on forming some kind of bond with the animal. How unsuccessful she's been at it. She wants to change the subject.

"How long has it been since there even was a phoenix?" Raqia asks.

"It's hard to say," Elsa answers. "False ones pop up now and then. The last documented one I know of was a few generations ago, but there may have been one since then in a less open part of the world." She shrugs gracefully. "Not every phoenix chooses to live in the public eye."

"But why wouldn't they?" Anabelle asks. "Being a phoenix is so special. Why wouldn't someone want to...celebrate that?"

Maybe because after a Plain life there might be just a tinge of bitterness, Raqia thinks, *especially if that Plain life was a long one.*

"I'm sure they have their reasons," Elsa says pleasantly. "But tell me about yourselves. Have you been friends a long time?"

"Since third grade," Raqia says. "Best friends." She smiles at Anabelle, who doesn't look back at her or say anything. That emptiness grows into Raqia's stomach.

After a moment, Elsa says, "Raqia, your affinity emerged recently?"

"Um, yes. Sunday afternoon. Most of the physical effects lasted only a couple of hours."

"She had fur growing out of these dark tattoos on her skin," Anabelle so helpfully volunteers, "that appeared really suddenly. *So* weird." She crinkles her nose and glances at Raqia's bare arms. "They all seem to be gone now."

Raqia glares at her. "That isn't really your story to tell, is it?"

"Excuse me." Anabelle's face is turning a little red, her voice straining to be civil. "Were you planning to hide it from people?"

"What exactly is going on here?" Elsa asks.

"No, I wasn't," Raqia says. "But it's my affinity—"

"And not mine," Anabelle says curtly.

"Ladies, I think maybe we should—"

"No," Raqia says loudly to Anabelle, her indignation growing by the second. "*Not* yours, because you still don't have one yet!"

Anabelle's gasp perforates the quiet in the wake of Raqia's outburst. After a moment, Elsa says quietly, "It's very clear that the two of you have some unresolved feelings about all of this. Why don't we spend just a minute taking some slow, deep breaths? It might help you avoid saying something you can't take back."

Anabelle turns to Elsa. "Rocky's a wolf."

Elsa stills. She recovers quickly, but Raqia sees the brief shadow of fear in her eyes.

Of course, she thinks. *Because who* doesn't *think the wolf affinity is a problem?* Well, of course Eddie doesn't. Not that he's here right now.

"Are there any others with the wolf affinity in your family?" the counselor asks.

Raqia shakes her head.

"That must have been a surprise when your affinity emerged."

"I'll say," Anabelle mutters.

Elsa says, "Would you like to talk about it?"

"No, but thank you," Raqia says, standing up. "I appreciate it, Ms. Elsa, but I think I need to leave." She casts a look down on Anabelle. "If our situations had been reversed, I wouldn't have treated you this way."

"Right," Anabelle sneers.

Raqia's shock at her comment, and what it likely means for the strength—or weakness—of their friendship, radiates through her whole body, making the hair on her arms prickle.

"Honestly, Anabelle," Raqia seethes, "you're being completely unreasonable. It's not my fault you didn't get your affinity this weekend, or that I did. So quit acting like a child."

"You don't like my behavior? Then go complain to Eddie, because *I don't care.*"

"How is this about him?"

Elsa clears her throat. "Who is Eddie?" she asks gingerly.

"He's the one who stole my best friend."

"He didn't *steal* me. I'm not a *thing* that can be taken."

"Whatever. You clearly belong to him now, not me."

Raqia is so stunned by Anabelle's bizarre take on the situation, she stomps out of the conference room, slamming the door behind her.

15

R AQIA IS LESS THAN five minutes from home when she feels the buzz of a text come in. It's from Anabelle. *Finally.* Raqia's expecting an apology, or at least some explanation for her friend's rudeness in the conference room. What she gets is not that.

I told Taita.

That's all it says, but there's only two things it could mean: either that Raqia is dating Eddie now, or that Raqia has gotten the wolf affinity. Both are unfair; Raqia should be able to decide when and how to tell her grandmother about both of those things. Preferably when she has them figured out in her own mind. Anabelle has had temperamental episodes in the past, but now her spite has rocketed to a new level.

Raqia hits the call button to try and talk to Anabelle directly, but it goes to voice mail. She tries texting: **what exactly did you tell her?**

No response to that, either.

Raqia speeds up her walk and goes to the Fosters' house instead of her own. She doubts Anabelle is there yet, but maybe she will be. Or even if she isn't, maybe her mom will be and Raqia can call from their house line, since Anabelle is less likely to ignore a call if she thinks it's from her mom. Raqia knocks on the front door and waits for a few minutes, but there's no answer. No car in the driveway. Out of desperation she tries the doorknob but it's locked.

Of course it would be, with no one home.

She's hot and cold at the same time, the queasy feeling she's coming to recognize as anxiety fermenting in her gut. She tries calling Anabelle again; it goes to voice mail almost immediately. Who knows when she'll get home?

Raqia can't put this off any longer. She crosses the street and enters her own front door. Taita is sitting at the kitchen table with a glass of iced mint tea and her book of crossword puzzles. She looks up when Raqia enters.

"Hi, Taita." She approaches carefully, as if her grandmother were the skittish creature in this scenario. "How...was your day?"

"All right, habibti." She folds her hands on top of her book. "Are you still feeling better? No sickness anymore?"

Raqia shakes her head. "All better."

"That is good." She gestures to a cookie tin on the counter. "I made ma'amoul today, if you'd like some."

"I'd love some." The butter cookie stuffed with dates and walnuts, covered in powdered sugar, is a special treat, usually reserved for holidays and birthdays. Raqia takes two from the cookie tin and puts them on a napkin.

"Come sit." Taita's smile is pinched but genuine.

Raqia sits across the table from her grandmother and holds up the half of a cookie she hasn't eaten yet. "So what's the occasion?" She's almost afraid to ask.

"You tell me."

She has no way of knowing what Anabelle revealed, and if she assumes it's one secret and it turns out to be something else, she'll be giving away more than she wants to before she's ready. Quite a creative punishment from someone who's supposed to be her best friend.

"I guess Anabelle told you, didn't she?" Maybe Taita will give it away, if Raqia can get her talking.

Her grandmother only nods and takes a sip of her tea. But she doesn't look...mad.

"I was hoping she would let me tell you myself, on my own time."

"Why would you wait to talk to me about this?" Taita looks almost offended.

"I guess I was hoping I could...I don't know, think about it some more first. I mean, it all just happened this weekend, and I'm still trying to figure out what I think."

Taita shrugs. "What is there to think about? You must have known I would find out. We live in the same house!" She tosses up her hands in exasperation. "You act as if I have never experienced anything, habibti."

But Taita hasn't experienced becoming a wolf before, and she sure doesn't like the wolf affinity very much—Eddie notwithstanding. Now Raqia isn't sure what Taita's expecting her to say.

"What...um, what exactly did Anabelle tell you?" Raqia puts the other half of the cookie in her mouth to give herself time to think of an answer, while she's chewing, to whatever her grandmother says next.

Taita cocks her head at Raqia. "How many things are you hiding from me?"

Not the way I was hoping this would go, Raqia thinks as she chokes the crumbly cookie down. "I'm not hiding anything, Taita."

"Then start talking, habibti." Her voice is firm, but loving.

Raqia sighs. Maybe Anabelle doesn't know that she and Eddie are together now. Maybe, in her insecurity, she's just assuming Raqia likes him better after the way Anabelle acted this weekend. So this must be about her affinity—which Anabelle is clearly pissed about for some insane reason.

Raqia is going to have to tell Taita sooner or later, anyway, and now she just wants to get it over with. "Okay. It started Saturday night. I thought maybe my being sick had something to do with it, because I woke up in the middle of the night and saw these...things all over my skin and then passed out. But it turns out that was just a dream." A weird dream. A prophetic dream. But she doesn't have time to parse that out now.

Taita's brow is furrowed, her eyes showing a confused concern. "A dream?"

"Yes, but then Sunday when I went over to Anabelle's house—"

"To see Eddie as well, yes?"

"Well, yes, of course he was there. And he said he had these...they were like tattoos that disappeared. Mandalas, on my skin."

"*Tattoos?*"

Oh, Taita doesn't like that at all. "*Like* tattoos, but not really." She pushes up her sleeve and shows her grandmother her unblemished skin. "See? Already gone. I ended up getting them over at the Fosters' house, but they lasted only a few hours. Eddie waited with me at the park down the street until they were gone. The fur, too."

Taita's face has gone bloodless. She hesitates, as if trying to decide what to ask first. "And were you and Eddie at the park alone? Until dark?"

"Well, sort of—"

"I knew that you would find a boyfriend at some point," Taita says. "And I am not sorry you picked Eddie. He is a kind boy, and he has liked you for a long time. I wondered why it took so long." But her face is still a map of worry.

Oh, so Anabelle told her that Eddie and Raqia were...a thing now. "So you don't mind if I...date him?"

Taita begins to shake her head but then stops. "Tell me about the mandalas and the *fur*." Her stern voice makes it clear Anabelle didn't tell her about the wolf affinity messily bursting out of Raqia at their house.

But now Raqia basically has. *Damn.* She really wishes Eddie were here to smooth this over. How is she going to explain this to Taita without her becoming upset?

Taita clears her throat, a whistling *whoo* underneath the scratch, and shakes her feathered hair sharply out of her eyes. Drums her sharp fingernails on the table. "I am waiting."

"My...affinity," Raqia mutters. She can't look her grandmother in the eye. Panic builds in her chest, the tightness rumbling into a low growl that she chokes to keep down.

But Taita hears it anyway. "*What* animal, habibti?" Her voice is quiet, crisp.

This really isn't how Raqia wanted to tell her. Eddie was going to be here with her, showing off his very best manners and holding Raqia's hand. Making jokes with Taita in that easy way of his. Charming her so she would see there's nothing to be afraid of. Eating ma'amoul with them. Raqia picks her second cookie up and accidentally crushes it in her fingers.

Taita gasps. Raqia wants to cry. All the cautionary tales she's grown up on, of her mother's death, of the Beiruti packs, the endless admonishments to Eddie, and then Taita checking up on him after that liquor store robbery—

All of it adds up to a very desperate sum: that Raqia has become the thing her grandmother fears the most.

"I'm so sorry, Taita. I think I'm a wolf."

Then she bursts into tears, that damn growl underpinning her sobs, and runs into her bedroom, slamming the door behind her, before Taita can say a single word.

Before she can tell Raqia just how much more broken her heart can be.

16

RAQIA LOCKS HERSELF IN her bedroom before Taita can stop her, but her grandmother isn't having that.

"Habibti, let us talk about this now," Taita says through Raqia's door. Her voice is weary, wary, but also tender. Fragile.

"I don't want to," Raqia answers.

"But we cannot ignore this," Taita's voice continues. "I know you are upset, and you must have questions."

How can Taita sound so calm? Raqia has become her grandmother's worst fear.

She texts Eddie: **Taita knows about my affinity. Anabelle trapped me into telling her because apparently she hates me now. I don't know what to do**

He doesn't text her back, but it's probably because he's in class right now or at football practice. He'll be back home in a few days. Surely he'll call her tonight, too. But she really wishes he were here now. None of this turned out like they planned Sunday night.

"You must not lock yourself away like this. Come out and let us talk." There's comfort in her voice.

Raqia wants to go to her, wants to fall deep into one of her hugs, eat ma'amoul and be excited about getting her affinity, about Eddie. She wants to giggle and make dreamy plans about how different school will be, about the friends she will have, about what her future might look like. Things she imagines girls her age would normally do after getting a boyfriend and an affinity all in one weekend.

The list of things that are wrong about Raqia's situation tower over her, casting an anxious shadow over all she had hoped this time in her life would have been.

"Raqia, it is time to come out of your room now." Taita's voice has grown firmer, but not angry, not cold. It's coaxing. "You do not need to be afraid."

And that's really what this is about, Raqia's fear. Fear of what Taita will think, what Anabelle will do, what dating Eddie will be like, even who she can sit with now at lunch at school. She's reminded of the fear Elsa talked about having, how it had held her back for so long.

Raqia sniffs and wipes her cheeks dry. Eddie still hasn't texted her back. Anabelle hasn't either, not since her message on the way home from school.

A surge of indignant anger heats Raqia's blood again at the callous ambiguity of that text. She's not even sure how good an idea it would be to try and talk to Anabelle right now. She doesn't know what she would do, how she might lash out at her, what she would say and regret later, and then be utterly without any close friends for the second half of high school.

But also, part of her is tired of being the one who always smooths things over, who always averts confrontation. She never wanted to upset the apple cart before, either out of fear of reprisal or fear of being considered too difficult to put up with. But now, she's spoiling for a fight, and she doesn't know if it's her affinity settling in or if she's just finally hit a threshold of too much hiding in the margins. And if she has the kind of fight Anabelle seems to be inviting, she's not sure they can come back from it. Catastrophic thoughts begin spiraling around in her head like a tornado, echoing in a roiled stomach. She tries deep breathing, like Eddie said to do.

Taita's voice again: "Habibti. You cannot stay in there forever."

Yeah, true. She has to admit she won't get over her fears locked up in her bedroom. She growls a little to herself—is that something she's going to do a lot now?—and heaves herself up from the carpet, then opens the door. Taita is still standing there, an expression of love in the undercurrent of her worry. That combination disarms Raqia's vitriol, and she hugs Taita fiercely. Lets her grandmother's arms hold her, warm her.

"It will be all right, habibti," she murmurs into Raqia's hair.

"How?" Raqia's voice is muffled by Taita's soft shoulder.

"Oh, because it has to be."

Raqia looks up. "What do you mean?"

"You must choose the kind of person you will be. This is the same every day. You had to choose last year what kind of person to be, and also when you were a child. And you will make this choice always, every day, for your whole life."

"But you hate wolves!"

"No, I worry about those with the wolf affinity who end up in the news reports. Those who choose wrong."

"But you worry about Eddie," Raqia insists. "You called his house Saturday morning to find out whether he had robbed a liquor store! Which is crazy—he would never do something like that."

Taita sighs heavily. "I know this, I know."

"Then why did you call him?"

"Because, habibti, I worry for him, too. I worry about him and Anabelle as if..."

Raqia clocks the tremor in her grandmother's voice, like she's about to go back on her words. "As if they were your family, too," she finishes.

Taita nods. "I admit, yes." She pulls something out of her pocket and places it in Raqia's palm, covers it with her own. Her skin is soft, even despite the gnarled veins traversing the back of her hand. She has given Raqia another ma'amoul wrapped in a napkin. "And now, perhaps, I will worry about Eddie even more." She smiles slowly, causing Raqia to smile a little bit back.

Raqia nibbles at the cookie, savoring the sweetness of the minced dates and the bright crunch of walnut, the buttery crumble of its shell. Taita leads her back to the living room, and they sit on the couch.

"Now tell me what all you are afraid of," she says, but Raqia doesn't want to. That's too much, too soon. When she doesn't respond, Taita continues, "Or maybe just one little thing. The first reason you locked yourself in your room."

One thing is perhaps not too much. "I was scared you'd be mad."

"About Eddie? No, I knew you would start dating someone eventually. At least I know Eddie already."

That's actually a relief. Taita started telling her stories in middle school about how Lebanese girls should wait until they were eighteen to begin dating, which always seemed extreme but also irrelevant, since no one had ever shown much interest in dating Raqia anyway. But now it looks like she doesn't have to worry about Taita's objections? This thing with Eddie is so new she isn't even sure "dating" is the right word for it yet. The homecoming dance didn't really feel like a date, not for most of the night.

Then she says, "I thought you'd be mad that my affinity was wolf."

"Ah." Taita is quiet a moment. She looks thoughtful. Then she purses her lips and pushes her round-framed glasses up her beaky nose. "Tell me, habibti, did you choose your affinity?"

"You know that's not how it works."

"But do *you* know that? How could I be angry at you for something you have no control over?"

"I guess maybe I thought you'd be mad in general. Mad at the situation."

"Well." Taita sighs. "Would I have chosen the wolf affinity for you?" She shrugs, and Raqia holds her breath, not sure how she will feel about any answer Taita can give. "I would not have chosen it, but I would not take it away from you if I could, either."

"But the Beiruti packs—"

"Oh, are you thinking of going there to join them?"

Taita's glare seems meant to be funny, and Raqia can't help laughing. "Of course not!"

"Well, then the Beiruti packs are not part of this circumstance, are they?"

"But they—" Even though Raqia doesn't remember her mother, not really, she can't say it out loud. *They killed her,* she thinks, and Taita somehow knows it's what Raqia is thinking.

"That was an act of random violence, habibti. She was not a particular target. Those wolves did not choose wisely."

And the subtext is more than clear: make the right choices, every day, and you can escape that violence yourself.

But how can she make the right choices when the affinity feels so violent inside of her? She thinks about Chuy, how she almost crushed him. And about the rabbit Eddie killed on that camping trip in middle school. How he now channels that violence into football. It isn't really gone. He even said himself that it takes an iron will to control his emotions.

Then Taita says, "I was surprised when Anabelle called me at lunch today."

So she'd already done it when Raqia showed up for their appointment after school. *And* she hadn't mentioned it. Raqia can't decide if this new detail makes Anabelle's behavior this afternoon worse or more understandable.

No, never mind. Her behavior sucked. That's all there is to it. Calling Taita and ratting Raqia out, accusing her—because that's what it felt like—during the meeting with Elsa, her cold attitude all morning—these aren't the actions of someone with Raqia's best interest at heart. Rage blooms within her like a desert weed, hot and prickly and inevitable.

"Do you know why she did this?" Taita's voice brings Raqia back into the calm of their living room.

Her grandmother has too keen an eye for Raqia to pretend there's nothing wrong between her and Anabelle. She might as well tell her the truth, or as much of it as she can guess at.

"Anabelle is angry with me, unfairly I might add, because of what happened this weekend."

"Which part of what happened this weekend?"

"I wish I knew. Maybe because I got sick at the dance and we had to leave early, cutting her time with Taylor short. Maybe because her brother likes me as more than a friend, and I like him back. Maybe because I got my affinity and she didn't. It could be any of those. It could be all of them."

Taita nodded. "Maybe because that affinity is the same thing her brother has and that makes her worry, and maybe she is now going to worry about you."

Okay, Raqia hadn't thought about it from that angle. It seems like a generous interpretation, given Anabelle's sudden hatefulness.

She considers their long friendship, the way they've clung to each other for years like barnacles. The way they've been each other's only close friend, defended each other, helped each other. All of that simply couldn't have been just desperation.

"Maybe you're right," Raqia mutters. She wants that, but the sting of her best friend's spite can't be ignored.

Ping. A text comes through, from Eddie: **hey, sorry I missed you earlier, can you talk now?**

Raqia must be smiling because Taita laughs gently. "Go on, habibti, go talk with him now. You and I will talk again later."

Raqia lets out a relieved exhale and puts her phone back in her pocket. "Thanks, Taita."

But before Raqia can stand, her grandmother gently places a taloned hand on her arm. "We will talk more later, yes? You will tell me more often how things are going?"

"Yeah," Raqia promises. She gives Taita a quick peck on the cheek and heads off to her room again, this time in a much better frame of mind.

17

T HE NEXT THREE DAYS at school are tense, to say the least.

Straining against her better judgment, Raqia confronts Anabelle at her locker on Wednesday morning with a low, uncomfortable growl and a quietly muttered, "Don't ever go behind me and tell my grandmother news that isn't yours to share."

Anabelle's eyes widen and then narrow like knives. "Are you threatening me, Rocky?" Her voice is a little too loud for such a public place.

"I am not," Raqia answers. "But right now you're being the worst friend in the world, and I don't deserve that."

"And I didn't deserve being kept in the dark by my best friend. Couldn't you have told me what was going on?"

What is this nonsense? Raqia learned about her affinity *in front of* Anabelle. "I don't even know what you're talking about."

Just as Anabelle is screwing up her face for a retort, Puppyface saunters down the hall toward them. "Hey, weird sisters," he says with a smirk and walks right up into their space, angling his body to edge Anabelle out of the conversation. "I hear you've joined the wolf side," he says to Raqia. He slowly looks her up and down, lingering on the books she's holding in front of her chest like he can see through them.

Anabelle snorts in disgust. "You're so gross, Luke."

He doesn't even turn to look at her. "I'm not talking to you, little Annie."

Raqia cringes inwardly. Anabelle has hated that nickname since fourth grade. No one uses it now, so either one of Anabelle's family members told Puppyface about it—unlikely—or he came up with it on his own. Not exactly original. Puppyface is a way better tag.

"Let me know if you have any questions about your new affinity," he murmurs to Raqia. "I'm happy to help."

"Go. Away," Raqia says. "I don't need or want anything from you."

He lifts his hand like he's going to brush her hair back behind her ear and she slaps it away faster than she ever thought she could move. Better reflexes indeed.

Puppyface just sighs like a dog and saunters back off. Raqia looks at Anabelle, whose face has gone red with seething.

"He's such a jerk," Raqia mutters.

Anabelle practically hisses, "No sympathy. Birds of a feather."

"What? What does that even mean?"

But Anabelle stomps off. The bell rings for class, and Raqia has to hurry to get to biology before lab really gets underway.

Thursday and Friday aren't any better. By the time the Friday afternoon dismissal rings, Raqia's had enough of Anabelle's pissy attitude, enough of Puppyface's leering, and enough of other random classmates suddenly trying to talk to her like they've been her friends all through high school. Even Alain and his beastly cohort have backed off the jeering in French class. And while Raqia isn't going to complain about the lack of randos heckling her, she feels unmoored by all of it, like the world has gone tail over teakettle.

But Friday night Eddie comes home. His game isn't until Saturday, so his coach is going to let him stay at his family's house that night instead of at the hotel with the rest of the team, as long as he's early to practice the next morning.

"That's great," Raqia says when Eddie calls to tell her he'll be home for dinner. He's on the bus, and she can hear the ambient noise of his teammates in the background. She's walking home from school. Alone, again. It's terrible having just her own intrusive thoughts for company, now that she and Anabelle are avoiding each other. "But your coach, he's just going to trust you like that?"

Eddie's laugh brings her to a better mood. "A few of us are from the Houston area, and we're all allowed to go home. It's like that in every city we travel to, if there's someone on the team from that place. Our families miss us, things like that. Besides, Coach knows where we all live, and believe me, he will come drag us out of our beds himself if we're late to practice." His voice is rich, deep, soothing against the backdrop of his teammates' raucous chatter, some bass-heavy music in the conversational distance. "He's a good leader, respected by the whole team." He's quiet for just a second, then he says, "Anyway, I figured you could come over for dinner, and then we could maybe go out for a while?"

"Go out," she repeats, her voice tinged with a shy smile. "Like, to a movie or something?"

"Maybe. I'd love to sit next to you in a dark theater for a couple of hours." His wolfish grin is *audible*. What is this new version of Eddie going to be like, really? Other than last weekend, she hasn't ever witnessed his romantic side. He dated some in high school, but he never rubbed her or Anabelle's noses in his popularity the way some older brothers might.

"I mean, that sounds like fun," she says. "But dinner. Your sister and I aren't speaking right now."

He sighs. "Still?"

"Things are as frosty as a polar bear's nose."

"Right. Okay." He's quiet for a few more seconds. "You know that's going to have to stop."

"I didn't start it!"

"I didn't say you did. Anabelle is very much at fault here, I get that."

"Have you talked to her?"

He snorts. "No. I tried texting her, but she isn't interested in hearing about this from me."

"She knows you'll take my side." As soon as she says this, she worries he won't. "I mean, you might."

"I'm not taking sides between my sister and my girlfriend."

Girlfriend. The word hangs in the pause like a column of bees, thick with honey and dangerous if disturbed. So Raqia says nothing.

"The problem is between the two of you," Eddie continues, as if Raqia's silence didn't even register. "So the two of you have to work it out. You know this. I won't be of any use and might actually make things worse if I step in."

"I guess." And really, Raqia *does* know he's right. She just wanted him to defend her a little bit. "Anyway, I'm not sure it's a good idea for me to come over for dinner. I doubt your parents want Anabelle and me fighting the whole time. And honestly, I don't have the stamina for it. This week has been awful."

"I'm *sure* you could handle it, Rocky," he says with affection. "But tell me about your awful week." It sounds like he's settling down into his seat on the bus. The noise around him is still there, but it doesn't prevent her from hearing *him*. It probably prevents his teammates from doing so, though.

Feeling slightly less self-conscious at that thought, she launches into all the details it was too troublesome to text him about during the week. She didn't want to seem whiny and thought it might come across that way over text. He interjects now and then with a sympathetic noise or a word or two of agreement, and somehow, that's enough, because by the time she gets home, she's feeling better. She doesn't know if that will last beyond the phone call, but for now it helps.

"I'm glad things were okay with Taita," he says, when she gets to the end of her saga. "I'm sorry I wasn't there with you, like I said I would be."

She shrugs, even though he can't see it. "It's okay. I'm glad it's done now."

"Yeah. Do you think she's going to give me a hard time about dating her perfect Lebanese granddaughter?" He's grinning again.

"Perfect, ha." She never has been. It's always been a scrabble just to feel good enough.

But not, she realizes, with Taita. Only around other people. Only at school.

"I know you're not eighteen yet, so she's probably secretly planning to claw my eyes out with those talons of hers—"

That makes Raqia laugh. "I doubt it. She might have some cautionary words for you—"

"Oh good, that'll be new and different."

She laughs again. "But she'll probably also give you some ma'amoul, too."

"Aw, that's sweet. But it isn't even my birthday."

Raqia loves that Eddie already knows this tradition, that he loves their food. That he respects Taita. He even calls her "grandmother."

"Anyway," he continues, "come over for dinner. Please. I miss seeing you."

"I miss seeing you, too," she says. If she and Anabelle can work things out, then the game tomorrow will be a lot less awkward and uncomfortable. And also, Raqia misses her best friend. Not just at school, but in every aspect of their lives they've shared for so long. "I'll think about it."

Ultimately Eddie persuades Raqia to come over without too much more convincing. When she gets to their house a couple of hours later, Anabelle answers the door and blocks the entry with a defiant stance.

"Do you need something?" she asks, hostility so torrid it practically curls her hair.

"Eddie invited me over for dinner."

"Plans have changed. We're not having dinner."

Raqia fights the urge to roll her eyes. She doesn't even growl, the excuse is so dumb. "Come on, Anabelle. Just let me in."

"No."

"Look, even if Eddie hadn't invited me for dinner—which he did, and which I accepted—you and I need to talk. I'm sick of avoiding each other. This is stupid."

"Stupid?" Her voice notches up an octave. "Are you calling me *stupid* now?"

"No, but freezing me out is. What are you so mad about? I have a theory, but you haven't even explained why you suddenly hate me now, after being best friends for eight years." She pauses to get her voice in check. "I deserve to hear it from you. Without that, I'm just left to think the worst."

"It's not like you haven't been keeping something from me!" Before Anabelle can say anything more about what that is, Eddie appears at the door.

"Hey, Rocky." His grin is infectious and makes her smile back despite the strife. "It's good to see you." His voice is low and inviting. Then he glares at Anabelle's blocking stance. He looks back at Raqia. "Why, pray tell, are you still on the porch?"

Then he reaches for her hand and pulls her gently past his sister and into the entry hall. Raqia resists the urge to shoulder-check Anabelle as she walks past her—that *won't* be helpful—but it's a close call. She sees Chuy sitting halfway up the stairs, but when she enters the front hall, the cat hurries the rest of the way up and disappears. Raqia looks away before Anabelle notices her looking at her cat.

Then Raqia's stomach flutters when it looks like Eddie might kiss her there, but he stops short, putting one arm around her shoulders in a tight hug and then just...not letting go. They look at each other, and when Anabelle groans, they look at her.

"Problem?" Eddie asks her.

"Definitely," Raqia answers—out loud, oops.

Anabelle gestures wildly toward their awkward side hug. "Do you have to do this here?"

"Do what?" Raqia asks, defensiveness creeping into her own voice.

"She knows how I feel about you," Eddie murmurs.

"And how is that, exactly?" Raqia thinks she knows, but easy endearments over text or on the phone aren't the same as being in the same room with him. She can't even explain to herself why that would be, either. It's not as if Eddie is a stranger to her. *This is just a strange...context,* she thinks.

His grin threatens to swallow his ears. "Tell you later."

"*Gross,*" Anabelle seethes.

"Get over it," he mutters.

"Both of you please stop," Raqia says, lapsing back into the well-worn role of peacemaker between the two siblings. "Anabelle, we need to talk."

"I agree," Eddie says. "Work it out. I'm going to go help Mom with dinner." He bounds off to the kitchen.

"You can't tell me what to do!" Anabelle shouts after him.

"Just tell me why you're so mad," Raqia says. She sits on the next-to-last step of the staircase, so Anabelle can't retreat upstairs. "I haven't done anything to you."

"You're dating my brother now. Does this mean you prefer him to me?"

Raqia rubs her temple. "That doesn't even make sense. I was never dating *you*. I still want you for my best friend. And this thing with Eddie—yes, okay, I like him as more than a friend." Saying it out loud feels natural, right. "Why can't both of those things be true? Why can't I have both of you?" That *doesn't* sound right, but her swirling emotions are threatening to overwhelm her and she's having trouble putting everything into words. "I don't understand why you're so upset at the idea that Eddie and I would—"

"You can't understand because you don't have any siblings yourself," Anabelle says, the acid in her voice burning the skin off Raqia's heart.

That's low. "And *you* have no idea," she says through gritted teeth, "what it's like for what little family you have left to be in *another fucking country*. You have two parents, a brother, and the comfort of knowing you were born here, speak your native language, and have never felt displaced. You've lived in this city—in this *house*—your whole life! You're so—you're just so—insensitive."

Anabelle just shrugs.

When she can speak without wanting to scream, Raqia continues, "Just because I have my affinity now, it doesn't change me. I'm still—" She takes a deep breath. How many times have they talked about this over the last few years? All of their anxieties about being Plain, all their reassurances that affinities can come at any time, without warning, on no set schedule. The faith that an affinity doesn't change a person's fundamental nature, repeated to each other like a mantra when Eddie became a wolf. "Remember that vow you made us take in ninth grade? *Best friends forever.* Do you honestly think I would go back on that?"

The implied accusation lands: Anabelle looks away, nibbling on her lower lip and fidgeting her foot.

Raqia continues, "That promise meant something to me. It still does."

Finally Anabelle says, so quietly Raqia isn't sure she's heard her correctly, "I think we should hive off."

"What exactly are you talking about?" Raqia can feel that low growl building in her chest. Subtle kitchen noises prick at the edge of her hearing.

"You've clearly found other friends at school."

"A bunch of people treating me differently isn't the same as making friends, and you know—"

"And I'm exploring other options too."

"Like what? The Plain Isn't Pain club?" Like the church youth group before that, the softball team before that, the drama club before that? "How long is that going to last?" Raqia doesn't mean to sound dismissive or angry, but she can hear it in her voice and see the hurt on Anabelle's face.

"Yes, I'm in the club now." Another pause. "Taylor supports my decision."

Just how much of this is about the boy who was so scared of Anabelle's brother that he stood her up for homecoming?

Eddie comes to the doorway and says, "Dinner in five."

Anabelle's glare at him could melt lead. So no, it can't *all* be about Taylor.

"Thanks," Raqia says.

He gives her a little salute and disappears again, not even acknowledging his angry sister.

"Okay," Raqia says coolly, "well, I'm glad you and Taylor are talking again."

Anabelle scoffs and rolls her eyes. "Yeah, no thanks to Eddie for coming back home this weekend."

Suddenly Raqia wonders whether Anabelle knows her brother is planning to move back more permanently.

"And now *you*..." she continues.

"What?" Raqia is just confused. What does Anabelle suspect her of now?

"Well, Taylor is hardly going to want to date a girl whose brother *and* best friend are *both* wolves. The world is just too scary a place for that."

Raqia can't hold in her sarcasm. "I guess it's a good thing you don't have a predatory affinity then, isn't it."

Anabelle's eyes narrow. "That was really unkind. I guess maybe this is your true nature, finally coming out. So glad you're finally being honest. We're done."

The numbness in Raqia's arms and legs threatens to buckle her under; thankfully she's still sitting on the stairs, or she might've stumbled where she stood. Little pinpricks of alarm, a subtle ringing in her ears. Despite Anabelle's constant search for a group to be part of, Raqia always enjoyed primacy in the hierarchy of Anabelle's regard. Now, though, it seems she's throwing over their long friendship—for a boy? Two boys, maybe, since she thinks Eddie *stole* her somehow. She hears herself mutter the word *ridiculous* without meaning to.

"I'm not ridiculous, I'm careful. I have self-preservation."

Raqia feels like she's swimming in poisoned cotton. "That doesn't even make any sense."

A car horn honks outside. Eddie comes to the doorway again.

"Whatever," Anabelle says. "That's my ride."

"Where are you going?" Raqia asks.

"Out."

"Who's out there?" Eddie asks.

"Some of my *new* friends." Anabelle's voice does haughty a little too well. "I'm going to dinner with *them*."

Replacements. Already.

"Whatever. More prime rib for us." Eddie goes back to the kitchen.

"This isn't over," Raqia says. Not just the conversation, but the friendship. It *can't* be over, even if right now it feels like it. She's stuck in her spot, unable to stand or prevent Anabelle from grabbing her purse, prevent her from walking out the door without saying another word.

When the front door closes, more loudly than necessary, Eddie comes back across the hall and holds his hand out to Raqia. "Come on," he says softly, "let's eat."

"I don't understand," she says. Anabelle's departure feels like more than jealousy.

"What's there to understand?" he says. "She needs time to cool off. Time to adjust to all of this."

All of this. All of her, Raqia. And it doesn't feel like Anabelle has any intention of doing that. She takes Eddie's hand and lets him lead her into the other room for dinner.

His parents are kind and welcoming, looking just as happy to see her as they ever have been. They're either oblivious to what's happening between her and Anabelle or—more likely—ignoring it because...why? Why do they look so unconcerned? Raqia's world is molting with nothing but raw, fragile skin underneath.

She sits down at this table where she's had dinner hundreds of times before. The Fosters envelop her in the same friendliness she's always had from them, with the added warmth of Eddie's affection underpinning it all.

And yet she feels, now, more like a stray than ever.

18

AFTER DINNER, EDDIE AND Raqia help clear away the dishes, and then Mrs. Foster shoos them out of the kitchen.

"Go, relax, have fun."

Mr. Foster, who has already settled himself in the living room in front of the television, calls out, "Not too much fun. You still have a game tomorrow."

Eddie closes his eyes and takes a deep breath before answering, "No worries, Dad. We're just going to a movie." Then he ushers Raqia toward the front door.

"What movie?" she asks.

Eddie smiles and shrugs. "Who cares?"

She smiles shyly back, every nerve ending singing at the idea of going on an actual date with him, while her gut simmers with frustration, hurt, and worry over the state of her friendship with Anabelle. She doesn't want to think about her right now; dwelling on their fight will ruin her time with Eddie, and she doesn't deserve that. Neither does he.

Eddie closes the door behind them and twirls his dad's car keys around his finger. "Let's just go out somewhere, unless there's actually a movie playing you want to see. Then we can totally do that." He holds the passenger car door open for her, and when she climbs in, he closes it before walking around to the driver's side. The special attention makes her feel incandescent.

When he gets in, she says, "I can't think of any interesting movies out right now." Then she smiles at him again. "But that doesn't mean we can't go to one."

He kisses her and everything else that came before recedes into a background of distant noise. When he breaks away, she takes a breath.

He says, "Let's start with ice cream and see where the evening takes us."

Anything you like, Eddie. "Okay, sure."

He starts the car and backs out of the driveway.

As they leave their neighborhood, he steers the car with his left hand and holds hers with his right. His skin is warm, the palm of his hand a little callused. At first the constant contact feels strange, but within minutes, holding hands with him feels natural, something she might have done a hundred times throughout their childhood. She must have, at some point, when they were growing up.

She asks, "Are you nervous about the game tomorrow?"

He shakes his head. "Not about playing. I can play football in my sleep. It's not that hard."

It looks hard, though. Painful. But Eddie doesn't seem to mind the physicality of it. On the field, he always looked like he enjoyed it. Maybe he leaned into it in high school because it was easy to, but he was careful not to let the people who really knew him believe that was his whole personality. Raqia is starting to appreciate how big a challenge that must have been.

"And Coach said I'm starting, so that should make my dad happy." There's a flatness in his voice.

"Have you talked to your parents yet about transferring schools?"

"Not yet. I want to wait until after the game. If we win, Dad'll be in a better mood. If we lose, maybe I can convince him pro football isn't the path ahead for me." He clears his throat. "I'll probably wait until I'm back at school, honestly, in case he blows up. Or maybe just wait till I have decisions in hand from both schools. Dad's growly roars are not fun. I don't like being on the...receiving end of it, no pun intended."

Mr. Foster has never, to Raqia's knowledge, laid a hand in anger on either of his children—and surely she would've known if he had. But she has witnessed his temper once or twice, and it's pretty fearsome.

"Have you already heard back from either Rice or U of H yet? Do you know what your chances of getting in are?"

"I'm a transfer, so it's a little easier than being in a giant pool of graduating seniors." He smiles at her. "I like my chances at both."

Of course he does. Has he ever felt inadequate? But she says, "They're both really good engineering schools."

He nods. "Two of the best in the country."

"What kind of engineering do you want to do?"

"Anything is fine, but probably biomedical. Being close to the Med Center will help, too."

"Your dad has to appreciate that," she says. The Texas Medical Center, located literally across the street from Rice, has most of the best hospitals in the world. She feels a small frisson of pleasure at Eddie's ambition. He's smart enough to do all of this; it's something she has always admired about him.

"Theoretically, he will. *Paying* for college is the tricky part. I don't think I realized until this year how much he counted on my getting a full athletic scholarship."

"Can you not get that as a transfer student?"

"It's a lot harder. They're not going to love seeing that I turned down a full ride after three months. But I can probably get something. If I play well this quarter, my chances at looking valuable to a new university go up."

"What about your transcript?" If his grades aren't stellar, that will make a private school like Rice a farther stretch.

"Raqia." He looks at her as if she has asked a foolish question. "My grades are exceptional." He winks, then murmurs, "That's not hard, either."

"How easy it is for you. I'm so impressed." She can only barely keep the annoyance out of her voice. It's not that she isn't happy for him, but not everyone enjoys the kind of convenience in life that Eddie has had.

"Hey, you're not exactly bad at school." He parks in front of the ice cream shop and looks seriously at her. "I watched you coach my sister through how many math classes? And you've always been good at English and history."

"Good enough, I guess." She shrugs. If only she had been as good at other languages. Reading and talking about books is fine. Mastering the language of the country you're from when you leave it during the time you learn most of your foundational vocabulary is not. But she doesn't want to bring the mood down, so she squeezes his hand and smiles. Gestures toward the shop they've parked in front of. "So, ice cream?"

He grins and kisses the back of her hand that he's holding before letting it go. "Yep, come on."

She opens her car door before realizing he's coming to open it for her, so she gets out and immediately takes his hand as they walk in. She doesn't want him to think she didn't appreciate his gesture.

The line at the counter is slow, so Eddie ducks them into the photo booth in the corner while they wait. It's silly and fun posing for the four shots in that tiny space, and when the prints come out, she marvels inwardly at how happy he looks snuggling next to her, kissing her cheek, just holding her. It feels like half of all the close friendship she's ever known has suddenly expanded to cover her whole world. For the first time, someone else wants all of her, needs all of her, can't get close enough. And in exchange, all her volatility feels stable when Eddie is with her, like no matter how much of a tempest she has raging inside, he, himself, is enough to hold it in.

He splits the strip of pictures so they each get two of the images, and they put them inside their phone cases.

Eddie-on-a-date is a different beast from Eddie-who-lives-across-the-street. It's subtle. He still has the easy sense of humor and the inherent exuberance he's always had whenever he's in a good mood. But there's an undercurrent of extra attentiveness Raqia isn't used to. It's not like scrutiny—she's felt that for as long as she can remember, from Taita, from classmates, from bullies. But this? Eddie's dark eyes are like fire and water together: a burning heat she could drown in.

And he's more...tactile than before. It's not like he ever avoided contact, but now his touch is gentle, intentional. His long fingers tracing circles on her arm or the back of her hand. Playing with the end of her braid, curling her hair around his finger. Speaking in very low tones so she has to come closer to hear him, even with her sharpening senses, and then placing a soft kiss on her neck after whispering something in her ear.

She likes this new version of Eddie *very* much. She's just growing comfortable with how close he's sitting to her when loud voices on the patio outside overtake the music playing from the speakers above the ice cream cases. They look up from their rapidly diminishing cones to see Puppyface and B-Cad laughing and joking around with some of the people sitting outside. Eddie's expression darkens.

"I'm guessing you didn't know they would be here," Raqia says, starting to feel annoyed.

"Of course not." He looks back at her, surprised. "I would never invite them to a date with you." He angles himself more fully toward her and smiles. "Here, let's pretend we're deep in conversation." He props his elbow on the table and leans his head on his fist, giving his back to the front of the shop. "Come closer to me," he murmurs. When she leans her head closer to his, she realizes he has blocked her almost entirely from the view of anyone on the patio.

She smiles. "Do you think this will fool them?"

"Not sure. But I hope so." Then he looks at her lips and without thinking about it, she leans forward to kiss him. The bells on the shop door clanging stop her from doing it, though.

"Eddie!" B-Cad bellows and makes a howling sound.

Eddie closes his eyes as if trying to marshal his patience, then opens them. *I hate that,* he mouths to her. She just nods. Then he sits up straight and turns around, plasters a smile on his face that doesn't reach his eyes. "Hey, guys. How's it going?"

While B-Cad orders an ice cream, Puppyface pulls up a chair next to Raqia. Eddie's eye twitches at him.

"What are you adorable wolves up to this evening?" Puppyface drawls, kicking back in the chair like this whole party is his.

"Luke." Eddie's voice is stern. "What does it look like?"

"It looks like ice cream, my dudes," B-Cad says cheerfully as he pulls up a chair. Puppyface just looks at Eddie and shrugs. Arrogantly. Because of course he does.

"It's not just ice cream, *my dudes*," Eddie says. B-Cad looks...confused? "It's a *date*. Which you have now crashed."

"Oh." B-Cad looks genuinely contrite. Puppyface looks...like a jerk. B-Cad stands up. "So sorry, man. We didn't realize." He looks at Puppyface, who appears to be engaged in a staring contest with Eddie. "We should go." B-Cad tags his shoulder and looks at Eddie's scowl. "*Now*, dude."

"See you later!" Raqia says cheerfully to them both. Puppyface glares at her. A very low growl comes out of Eddie then, so low that Raqia wouldn't have heard it had she not already gotten her affinity.

But Puppyface hears it and heeds it. He stands. "See y'all at the game tomorrow." He smiles at Raqia but isn't, it looks like, brave enough to do more than that with Eddie there, with Eddie having essentially declared he and Raqia are a couple.

They leave, but the mood has deflated. Raqia thinks carefully about what she says next.

"You're coming back for all of them, aren't you. Not just Luke." It's not a question. "This is the real reason you want to transfer." She doesn't even feel hurt about it; she never expected Eddie was coming back for her. Or not *just* for her. And she would never have thought she was any part of his calculus a week ago.

Eddie slumps back in his chair. "I mean, I'm mostly coming back for me. I'm thinking about my future, what that looks like." He gazes at Raqia with a slight smile and toes the edge of her foot with his. "All aspects of that."

She can feel herself blushing. *Stop it,* she tells herself. *Cool your paws.* As if she could when he says things like that, when he looks at her like she means so much to him.

"But yes," he continues, "if I'm being honest, part of that future includes tempering Luke's influence on the other guys. They're not Big Bad material. Luke, on the other hand—"

"Is a criminal itching to hatch."

Eddie laughs a little. "Probably, yeah," he finally agrees. "It's a long way from now until graduation for all of them. They haven't decided on colleges yet. Their paths are still wide open." He sits back up and takes Raqia's hand. "I want to keep it that way."

"That's good of you." But *good* isn't really a strong enough word for this. It feels *noble*, but that doesn't seem right, either. The idea that Puppyface is likely going to be a big problem turns her stomach in the same way that thinking of the Beiruti packs when she was a child did. "Is it...safe for you?"

Eddie is thoughtful about his answer. "For whatever it's worth, Rocky, I've enjoyed influence." He looks down at their hands, suddenly seeming shy. Or maybe just humble. "I'd like to put it to good use."

Raqia just nods. She understands this impulse to want to do good, to want to make some kind of meaningful mark. She wants to make Taita proud of her, wants her father to notice her for good reasons. She wants to feel like she belongs. Eddie, though—

Well, everyone has always implied he had leadership potential. This was mostly confined to the context of his academic and athletic pursuits. But what if it could be more?

She can envision a pack coalescing around Eddie. With his charisma, he can hardly stop it. Thinking about the way he commanded the room here tonight, even Puppyface not really challenging him...

She has to take a deep breath. Maybe a pack has already formed.

"You ready to go?" he asks. "It's not late enough yet for us to have been to a movie." He grins. "We don't have to go home *just* yet. There's always the plaza over at CityCentre."

A relaxed, open-air green with fountains and restaurants and shopping built up around it. And yes, a movie theater, if they wanted to catch a late show. This time of night, it won't be so busy, even with the Friday evening dinner crowds. They can be anonymous there.

"Sure." She puts on a smile. "That sounds fun."

And walking out of the ice cream shop arm in arm with Eddie feels...inevitable.

It's not a long drive to CityCentre. Eddie is quiet for several blocks. Raqia squeezes his hand.

"Is everything okay?" she asks, suddenly worried that it isn't.

"Yeah, I'm just thinking about Luke. What can turn him away from the dark side. The head coach I have right now, he's really good at mentoring. He can handle even the biggest cretins on the team without any apparent effort. I'm trying to pay as much attention to how he does it as I can before I leave."

"Do you really want to leave that team, then?" Raqia feels a little tremor go through her as they stop at a red light. "What if your next coach isn't that good—"

"Raqia." He's looking very intently at her and his hold on her hand feels possessive, somehow urgent. "Literally nothing could convince me not to come home at this point."

That feels a lot more serious than she's expecting, even if she can't really say why his fervor surprises her. It's not...bad, or upsetting. It's just...a lot.

"Okay," she says quietly. "I get that." She smiles back at him and he starts driving again. After a minute that feels like ten, she asks, "Do you know what Anabelle meant when she accused me of keeping secrets from her?"

"She said that?"

Raqia nods. "At first, I figured she meant getting my affinity, but that doesn't really make sense. I mean, she was in the room when it happened."

They've arrived at the CityCentre parking garage and Eddie drives up a couple of levels to find an open spot. When he stops the car, he exhales heavily. "I assume she means us."

"But that's also new."

"She...hmm. She started to get suspicious Saturday after the dance, about...I guess the way I was acting toward you, the way I got annoyed with her. And then she saw us Sunday night, kissing in front of your house. Or, 'making out on the lawn,' as she put it in her incredibly dramatic way." He rolls his eyes. "She confronted me about it two seconds after I got home this afternoon." He gets out of the car and walks around to get Raqia's door.

"If she thought we'd been hiding that from her for a while, that would explain her hostility."

"I imagine so."

She's still processing this information as they walk down to the street level and find their way to the plaza. Even though it's well past the time when the dinner crowds are around, there are still people socializing on restaurant and bar patios and some kids playing a late-night soccer game on the green. Eddie and Raqia find a place to sit near the corner of the fountains. He spoons himself around her on the wide, square bench as they watch the colorful, synchronized waterspouts and listen to the ambient sounds of people enjoying the cooler evenings of October in Houston. The lighting in the plaza is low, and there are enough people around that no one will give them a second look.

Raqia sits cross-legged in front of him and leans her back against the solid wall of his chest. He rests his hands on her knees, then on her thighs. Her senses are already filled with him when he murmurs, "I miss you so much when I'm at school, Rocky. The last six weeks have been rough."

"Last six weeks?" She had no idea he was interested until the night of the homecoming dance.

"I didn't want to say anything before. I mean, I was leaving."

"Before when? You mean during the summer?"

She can feel him nodding. He leans down and kisses her neck on the side where her braid isn't. She shivers, a good kind of tremble. Then he kisses her shoulder, then her neck again. She puts her hands on top of his, moves them back to her knees and holds them there, intertwines their fingers.

"Eddie."

"Hmm?" He doesn't move away.

She's enjoying this, but... "We're in public."

He sighs into her shoulder then lifts his head. "It's fine, Rocky. No one cares."

She looks around and it's true; no one seems to be watching them. "But I care."

A quiet laugh behind her, not mean-spirited. Indulgent. "Point taken." He hugs her. "Want to go somewhere less public?"

She really does. "I think there's a new documentary about penguins or something playing at the movies right now."

"That sounds fascinating." He stands and holds her hand while she climbs over the bench.

"Doesn't it?"

He just grins and slings an arm around her while they walk to the theater. He buys them tickets for a pod in the last row, and they slip in barely two minutes before the last showing begins. There's almost no one else in the little auditorium.

She pushes up the armrest between their seats as the lights go down and snuggles next to him.

"Just to be clear, Rocky," he whispers, "are you actually interested in seeing this movie?"

She reaches up and kisses him softly, pulls back. "I couldn't care less about it."

Good thing, too, because they don't watch it at all.

19

AT THE GAME SATURDAY afternoon, Raqia sits with Eddie's parents. That's not entirely awkward, since it's not like they don't already know each other well. And both Mr. and Mrs. Foster seem perfectly content that Eddie and Raqia are now dating.

Mr. Foster has insisted that Anabelle attend the game, too, to support her older brother. The fury radiating off of her threatens to melt the bleachers they're sitting on. She sits on the opposite side of her parents from Raqia, and that *is* awkward. Mr. Foster pays little attention to this unusual circumstance, but Mrs. Foster is a lot more observant of her children's social patterns.

"What is going on with you two girls?" she asks, when they've settled into their seats and Mr. Foster has gone down to the concession stand for snacks. The silence in the back seat of the car on the way to the game was profound. Raqia just stared out the window while Anabelle read Bible verses she already had memorized on her phone.

Neither of them answers at first.

"I'm waiting," Mrs. Foster says. "Come on, out with it."

Finally Anabelle huffs a beleaguered sigh and mutters, "Forget it, Mom. It's nothing."

Mrs. Foster actually laughs at that, a rippling sound as graceful as her posture. "Try again, honey. Whatever this is, it's not *nothing*."

"Just leave me alone!" Anabelle bursts out and stands up.

"Where are you going?" her mom asks.

"To the bathroom! Is that okay?" She stomps away.

Mrs. Foster regains her composure more quickly than expected and turns to Raqia. "Would you like to explain it to me, then?"

"Honestly, Anabelle hasn't really come right out and said what she's upset about." Raqia clears her throat unnecessarily. Should she tell Mrs. Foster everything?

Well, why shouldn't she? It's not like it can make Anabelle even angrier at her. It's not like it will make her stop being Raqia's best friend. She's already made those choices. And who knows? Maybe Mrs. Foster will have some advice. She *is* Anabelle's mother.

"Frankly, Mrs. Foster, Anabelle seems to be really upset with me over a bunch of things, all of which are beyond my control."

"I'm listening."

"She seems to think Eddie stole me from her, which doesn't even make sense, and she's mad that I got my affinity first, which I didn't ask for, and now apparently there's something about Taylor? But I'm not sure how I factor into that. Just because I'm wolfy now doesn't mean I'm dangerous, right?" She looks earnestly at Mrs. Foster's face, which bears an expression of both surprise and dismay. "And now Anabelle is finding new friends and doesn't want anything to do with me."

Mrs. Foster exhales loudly. "Well, that was a lot to take in, Rocky." She shakes her head as if to clear it. "First, though, I'm happy for you that you got your affinity. And are you saying it's the same as Eddie's?" Raqia nods slowly. "What a lovely coincidence." Mrs. Foster gives her a tight smile. "I think my daughter probably just needs time to adjust to so many new changes all at once. I imagine she's feeling left out and a little stung by all of it—though I agree, getting your affinity when you did is not your fault." She looks thoughtful for a moment. "You know, the two of you have been inseparable for so long, I don't think the foundation you have for your friendship can be shattered so easily. It's not necessarily a bad thing to branch out and make more friends."

Far from helpful advice, this feels like a platitude. An answer from a parent who's only half paying attention. Who maybe doesn't want to get that involved.

Raqia doesn't want to lose her best friend, even a little bit, even with how mad Anabelle is at her and how indignant Raqia feels about that. She hasn't ever had enough friends to think that the loss of an important one—her vital core friendship—could be easily remedied, that such a friend could ever be replaced.

Mr. Foster comes back then, stadium food in hand: a salmon taco for himself, a green salad for his wife, and cheese calzones for Raqia and Anabelle.

He smiles at them as he offloads the food and sits down. Then he looks around. "Where's my other daughter?" Raqia thinks it's sweet the way he always lumps her in with his children, even if the sentiment doesn't go very deep.

"Restroom," Mrs. Foster says, squeezing dressing from a plastic tube onto her salad.

Then the players take the field and the crowd begins cheering, including Mr. Foster, whose dogged focus will now be lost to anyone and everything but his son's performance in the game.

Raqia sees Eddie then, looking unusually fit in his uniform. He gazes up into the stands, helmet in hand, and catches her eye. Subtly blows her a kiss. She manages not to blush in front of his parents, but inside her a warmth bubbles up. *Mine,* a voice from somewhere deep inside her brain murmurs. It's a weird, intrusive thought, but she doesn't argue with it. Having someone to call her own in this way...she likes it more and more.

Eddie isn't replacing Anabelle, is he? No, that's not a thing. As, it seems, she has repeatedly said. But it feels good to have him to focus on when she suffers the sting of Anabelle's absence. Ironic, that, given how much having Eddie is bound up in Anabelle's absence in the first place. It's like a snake eating its own tail.

Said grumpy sister comes back, finally, with another girl in tow, someone from the Plain Isn't Pain club. Ramona, maybe? Raqia can't remember her name. Probably-Ramona sits on the other side of Anabelle from Mr. Foster and no one makes any introductions. Raqia assumes Mr. and Mrs. Foster must already know her, which means Anabelle has been having this new girl over to her house instead of Raqia. A slight burn pricks at the edges of her eyes, but she doesn't want to examine it and blinks it away.

Instead, she focuses on Eddie, on the aggression he shows only on the football field. He directs the entire offensive line from his position, calling plays and leading his teammates so naturally. She can imagine him leading his fanboys, directing them toward safer choices than the ones Puppyface might make. During a turnover, it's both a little frightening and a little exhilarating the way Eddie takes down one of the opposing team's players—clearly an upperclassman—so easily. She hopes there are scouts from both Rice and U of H in the stands watching him.

She's also completely surprised by how invested she is in this game. That's definitely never been the case before. She understands the cause, of course, but it still catches her off guard. She turns to make a comment to Anabelle without even thinking, but Eddie's sister isn't watching the field.

Anabelle has turned her attention and conversation toward her new friend, her back to Raqia, and stays this way for a long time. And even though Raqia tries to focus entirely on Eddie's absolute—and, surprisingly, *appealing*—dominance on the field, Anabelle's bright laughter at something Probably-Ramona has said skitters down her spine like a spider. In that moment, Raqia sees a bereft future for herself without a best friend, and suddenly her bones feel as hollow as a bird's.

Then Eddie gets tackled, violently—is he being *crushed?*—and people in the stands begin shouting. Mr. Foster himself starts yelling at the referee for some reason Raqia doesn't understand.

Get up, get up, please, she thinks, as if willing Eddie back to his feet, unhurt, with the force of her own fear. It takes just half a minute, but he slowly rises and...literally walks it off. The cheering deafens her and she can't feel her hands or feet from the adrenaline flooding her system. The crowd seems to both want him to be okay and also, maybe, want blood. And this feeling is just...awful. All of it, too intense.

The game, the noise of the crowd. Anabelle's disregard, Raqia's replacement sitting next to her. Raqia's own affinity coursing through her this past week, upending her carefully ordered routines and introducing such wild emotions. Even Eddie himself—drinking some water and then jogging back into the game as if nothing has just happened—and last night, moving on her in the dark theater in ways she hadn't imagined she would love so much—even he, right now, he *himself* feels too intense.

Anabelle lets out a heavy sigh and Raqia sees the furrows in her forehead, the white-knuckled clench of her hands ease as it becomes clear he's not hurt. She glances at Raqia—who knows whether by impulse or habit—then looks away. After a beat she continues her conversation with Probably-Ramona.

Anabelle accused Raqia of throwing her over for Eddie, of betraying their long friendship for him. It doesn't matter that she didn't do so at homecoming weekend.

If Raqia chooses him now, chooses him over Anabelle, she will have been right, regardless of the timing.

Mrs. Foster said that the foundation of the girls' friendship couldn't be shattered so easily, but what if Raqia doesn't do anything to protect it? From the way Anabelle is talking and laughing with her new friend—the way she used to do with Raqia, before last weekend—it's clear that if anyone is going to salvage this best-friendship, it's going to have to be Raqia.

And she doesn't see a way to do that in her present circumstances.

During a time out, Eddie takes off his helmet and looks back up in the stands at Raqia. Smiles, blows her another kiss.

But she's gone numb with awareness.

And it's breaking her heart.

20

R AQIA AGONIZES OVER HER horrible epiphany all day Sunday. More breaking news alerts of random violence in nearby cities—attributed to wolves because wolves are all anyone seems to think ever break the law—well, they don't help her anxiety.

So she avoids her phone and doubles down on her homework and chores, but in the background of her mind, she can't seem to let go of the catastrophic spiral. It intrudes on both her biology homework and folding her laundry. She cleans her bathroom and even her closet in an effort to distract herself from it, tries to drown it with loud music and deep breathing, but nothing helps.

And when Eddie calls her that night, the sound of his beautiful voice breaks her heart all over again.

"It means a lot to me that you were there at my game," he says.

"But why?" she asks flatly. "I'm not even into football."

"Maybe not, but you're definitely into me." His flirting, once so charming, is painful now. When she doesn't respond, he says, less confidently, "I mean, at least I thought you were…"

"I was." She clears her throat. "I am." But there's no buoyancy in her tone, and Eddie isn't an idiot; he can hear it and inhales sharply.

"Why does it sound like you're about to say something I won't like?"

It takes a moment before she can speak.

"Rocky, you're kind of scaring me. What's wrong? Can we switch to a video call?"

If they do, if she sees his face, she won't be able say it. "No, I can't right now." She takes a deep breath. "Listen, Eddie, I think this is…all just too much for me right now."

"What're you saying?" He sounds…frantic? "What's too much?"

"All of it, everything."

"I need more to go on, Rocky. Help me understand."

"I just don't think I can do this right now."

"Are you breaking up with me? Please wait a minute—"

"I don't want to, I really don't. But I'm overwhelmed right now."

He's quiet for just a beat too long. "Is this because of Friday night? Did I—? I mean, I thought you wanted—"

"No, that's not it," she says. "I did. This is not about making out in a movie theater." And truth be told, she doesn't know which of them was more the aggressor there.

"Okay…" He sounds relieved but confused. "What is it about?"

"I just need some time to figure out everything that's happening to me right now. Us, my affinity, school, Anabelle. It's all just…a lot." The way she's explaining it sounds really pathetic, but she can't seem to remember any of the reasoned arguments that have spun around like a vortex in her brain all day.

"I see," Eddie says quietly.

"Do you?" She's half afraid of his answer.

"It sounds like you want some space."

"Maybe."

"And my living in literally another city right now isn't enough space, I guess." He sounds hurt.

"It's not physical space I need."

"Then what?"

"I just need time. All of this has happened really fast."

"Did it?" Of course it doesn't feel fast to Eddie, not if he wanted her even during the summer. Not that she knew that. "So, what, you want me to back off?"

Putting it that way sounds so…harsh. And harsh isn't how she feels right now. But putting her feelings into words has never been so hard.

"Eddie, can you appreciate how many things have changed in my life in the past eight days?"

He's quiet a moment. Then: "Yeah, I can." A long exhale. "I guess you want to take a break, then."

"Take a break, not make one."

It's like she can hear him nodding, the gears turning in his brain. When he speaks again, he says, "For how long?"

Until I can get Anabelle back, she thinks, but she doesn't say it. "I just have some things to take care of, and it's probably best if I focus on them for a while."

"Things?"

She half smiles at his insecurity, so uncharacteristic, in spite of the little pieces of her heart shattered inside her chest.

"Important things, Eddie. And when they're settled—"

"Can I have you back?" A nascent hopefulness has returned to his voice like a bright undercurrent. It makes her smile, makes her bloom warm.

"Are you sure you want that?" Her tone borders on flirtatious; she can't help it.

"Rocky—*Raqia.* Please." Hearing her real name in his voice sends a pleasurable frisson all through her. He says, "I will *always* want that."

Her breath catches in her throat. She will always want that, too. She's just not sure she can have it.

The next day at school, Raqia gets both an English paper and a French test back. Both grades are in the basement, because of course she's spent most of her nights the last week on the phone with Eddie instead of doing her homework to her usual standards. When the French test lands on her desk and she sees the grade, her heart rate pulses higher and a sinking feeling hits her stomach. She crumples it in her hand without meaning to and then quickly smooths it out before anyone in her class can notice. This is not a pattern she can afford to fall into.

Raqia is already seated when Anabelle comes into math class. She's walking with Probably-Ramona, who hovers at the edge of their table while Anabelle unpacks her textbook and spiral. Probably-Ramona has apparently just transferred into their section.

"Hey," Raqia says tentatively to both of them.

"Hi" is Anabelle's flat, no-eye-contact response. Probably-Ramona just glares. Why, Raqia has no idea.

The teacher begins to settle everyone down and Anabelle's new friend goes to an empty table across the room.

The whole period is tense. It's clear Anabelle is struggling with the new material, and during problem practice time, Raqia's impulse is to offer her help, like usual. But Anabelle turns to Probably-Ramona, and when *she* can't help her, goes up to the teacher's desk. Fine. Raqia understands the material without difficulty and finishes her entire problem set before the end of the period. Less homework for her, yay.

When the bell rings at the end of class, Raqia tells Anabelle, "I broke up with Eddie last night."

She expects her to be surprised, maybe even to feel flattered. *You did that for me? I'm so sorry I was rude. I never want our friendship to end.* Maybe even tell her, *I've reconsidered and I love the two of you together.* Okay, that would be a stretch.

Instead, Anabelle barely looks at her. She says, "I know. I woke up to a monologue of angry, hurt texts from my brother this morning. Great job chopping his heart into tiny chunks and then blaming me for it."

"*What?* I didn't do that!"

Probably-Ramona is back at the side of their table.

"Did you or did you not cite me as a reason that you were 'overwhelmed'?" Her little air quotes are so obnoxious Raqia can feel her temperature rising. "And did you or did you not tell him that you need space because of it?"

"That is absolutely twisting what I said—"

"So now you're calling him a liar?"

"No!" She can't believe this is happening. "And since when are you his big defender?"

"My god, you're fickle," Probably-Ramona interjects, staring at Raqia with a smug little pout.

"I'm sorry, but who even are you?" Raqia asks.

"Ladies, is there a problem?" Their teacher is looking at them with raised eyebrows and a slightly concerned look on her face.

All three of them glance around at the now-empty classroom. Raqia's embarrassment at being disruptive launches into the stratosphere.

"Nope, just leaving," Anabelle says and snaps up her backpack. She marches out of the room with her *apparent new best friend*, leaving Raqia there to finish packing up her notes in silence.

"Anything I can help with, Raqia?" her teacher asks.

"I appreciate it," she answers quietly, "but I don't think so." She puts her backpack on and gets to the door as quickly as she can. "Sorry about the..." She gestures vaguely and walks away.

Raqia goes to the library during lunchtime; she doesn't want to think of it as hiding, but she's avoiding the cafeteria and everyone she might see there sitting with Anabelle who isn't Raqia herself. She's not really hungry, anyway.

At a table in the back corner, Raqia draws slow doodles on a piece of notebook paper while trying to sort everything out. Anabelle must have thought she and Eddie were hiding their...romance from her. Of course that would upset her, and rightly so. And if Eddie had feelings for Raqia even in the summer—suddenly, his increasing friendliness seems less like grown-up charisma and more like barely contained affection—well, Anabelle, living in the same house with him, having seen Eddie in dating mode before, would have picked up on his feelings in ways Raqia couldn't have.

But they never talked about it—Raqia didn't know there was anything *to* talk about—so Anabelle must have assumed, once Eddie came back for homecoming, there really was something there. Anabelle wouldn't have known Raqia and Eddie weren't carrying on some long-distance thing while he was off at school.

And yes, maybe all of this is silly and far-fetched. But that doesn't mean Anabelle wasn't imagining it.

Raqia takes out her phone and composes a long text to Anabelle. She explains that this thing with Eddie only just started at the homecoming dance, no matter what his hidden feelings may have been. That she wishes she and Anabelle could have gotten their affinities together, and that she wouldn't have chosen to be a wolf if she could've made a choice, but it's what she is and now she has to reconcile that with her family's old trauma. That she doesn't know how things are going to settle, but she's pretty sure she'll lose her father permanently when he finds out. That no matter what has happened between them over the years, Raqia still craves Anabelle's friendship, still wants what they had.

And then she adds that breaking up with Eddie was not something she wanted to do. That she hopes it isn't permanent.

In her third text, she says, **and I hope that's something you can get on board with, because ultimately it isn't up to you.**

She watches her phone to make sure all the texts have been marked as delivered. A few minutes later they're all marked as read.

No response comes.

She wants to text Eddie, too, but what can she possibly say now? Chastising him for getting mad at his sister wouldn't make things better, and she doesn't know what he actually said to her anyway. His feelings are his feelings; she's not going to deny him that any more than she would want him to deny her.

On the one hand, she wishes she hadn't hurt him. On the other, maybe this means his feelings for her run deep enough that she won't entirely lose him. She's just going to have to wait to find out, and that uncertainty hurts, too.

But she needs to settle into her affinity—which is still giving her wild mood swings sometimes—and figure out what it means for her relationships with her father and with Taita. She needs to get her anxiety under control. She needs to get her grades back on track. And, the biggest problem of all, she needs to get some sort of resolution with Anabelle.

As Raqia trudges home from school, she laments the fact that after a lifetime of always doggedly making the best choices she can, to be an obedient and dutiful granddaughter and a caring, giving friend...now, she can't seem to get any of it right.

21

Over the next couple of days, Raqia doubles down on her classwork. She'll have to start thinking about colleges soon, and while she doesn't have the luxury of choice for expensive private universities, her academic standing is excellent from a childhood and adolescence spent striving to make her grandmother proud and her father attentive. Or, it was excellent until she started dropping balls all over the place. But she can get it back. She just has to focus. She actually enjoys her studies most of the time. Eddie wasn't just flattering her when he observed that she was good at school.

She wants to call him.

This winter it will be time to start looking for internships that will make her college applications competitive. A month ago, she expected to be doing all of this with Anabelle; they would, ordinarily, have looked for internships together. But Anabelle has been utterly silent. She's been hanging out with the Plain Isn't Pain club—which, fine, it's great that Anabelle is embracing her current circumstance as something other than a social death sentence; Raqia loves that for her, really—and she seems to have kept up a counseling relationship with Ms. Elsa.

Raqia doesn't know all of this because Anabelle has told her, of course, but she isn't blind. She's seen her going into the conference room near the school office. She can see the people Anabelle eats lunch with and has also seen some of them hanging out at the Fosters' after school. It's hard to miss, given that Raqia's bedroom window faces their house, and that her hearing has grown much sharper since her affinity emerged. She's alerted to every noise that comes from their front lawn while she stays in her room, trying to study. She can only imagine the frustration Eddie felt when he first transformed, and how he must have had to shield his sensitive ears from her and Anabelle's childish squeals whenever they got excited about something. Her keener senses make her appreciate even more the self-control he developed as a teenager.

Maybe she could just text him.

Raqia herself tries eating lunch with Kirstin and Julie on Thursday, but it isn't ten minutes before they start asking her about Eddie. When she can't answer a question about his game schedule, Kirstin gives her a narrow look.

"Aren't you dating him?" she asks.

"I mean...not really..."

Julie stops her fork halfway to her mouth. "What does that mean?"

"Are you just friends with benefits?" The salacious look on Kirstin's face makes Raqia's stomach curdle.

"Um, no, we aren't—"

"So you're saying he's still single?"

Raqia's mood turns angry quickly. "Don't you have a boyfriend already?"

"Oh, it's not for me. I have a friend who's interested."

Julie gigglesnorts into her napkin. Well, that's not suspicious at all.

"He's not available." Raqia packs up her sandwich and chips to leave.

Is Kirstin laughing at her, too? She starts, "But I thought you just said—"

Raqia's quiet growl surfaces. "And I'm more likely to know what's going on with him than you, so I advise you to take my word for it."

As she leaves the cafeteria, her keen hearing picks up Julie's skeptical remarks and Kirstin's snide response. Raqia can feel her anxiety rising again, tinged with jealousy. She finds an open picnic table in the quad and plops there. Takes out her phone and texts Eddie.

I miss you

Regrets it instantly. What if he doesn't res—

I miss you too. And a big red heart.

And just like that, some of the nausea subsides.

He texts, **I'm trying to give you the space you said you wanted but it's hard**

I know, it is for me too

Then those three little bouncing dots of doom. Hover and disappear. Hover and disappear. She can't stand it.

Eddie, please just say whatever it is you're thinking. the suspense is wrecking me

A pause, and then he replies, **maybe space isn't what you need**

He is *not* going to tell her what she's feeling. **you're right. I need clarity. I'll answer anything you ask**

I just had lunch with Kirstin and Julie

okay? how was it?

Kirstin seems to be obsessed with whether you and I are dating. or, more specifically, sleeping together

um... Then no response for almost a solid minute. Finally: **that's weird**

why would she care? Raqia asks.

no idea. I don't know her very well

Raqia wants to see him. She can't even rationalize why, when she's the one who broke up with him. But the urge is so strong, she can't think about anything else.

can I call you? she asks. At least she could hear his voice.

I would love that. Heart-eyes smiling emoji. She smiles back at her phone. **but I just got into lab. can I call you tonight?**

She doesn't want to wait that long. But then the bell rings, calling her back to class, too. And at least her stomachache has mostly subsided.

I'll call you the minute I'm done with practice, I promise

She texts back: **I'd like that**

She thinks about sending him a heart, too, but stops herself. *Way to go on making him give you space,* she thinks, annoyed with herself. Can she be consistent for even a minute?

French is her last class of the day, and when she comes out of it, Puppyface is leaning against the lockers, waiting for her. She gives him the curtest of nods and moves quickly into the flow of traffic, hoping to lose him in the crowded hallway. She's unsuccessful.

"How's it going, Rocky?"

"Don't call me that. What do you want?"

"I heard you and Eddie broke up."

"Where'd you hear that?" Probably Kirstin and Julie. That stupid growl starts building again and her fingernails are just itching to slice someone up.

"Does it matter?" They've reached her locker now and she slams it open, begins exchanging books quickly, and then slams it closed. Puppyface doesn't leave her side. "Is it true?"

"There's a lot you don't know about the situation."

"Ooh, that sounds like a fun story." He edges closer to her in the throng of loud classmates. She heads for the exit doors as fast as she can. "Want to talk about it?"

"I do not."

He keeps pace with her all the way down the front steps of the building. A horrible thought occurs to her, that he's going to follow her home. She halts at the sidewalk near the bike racks. Now that they're outside, it's easier to hear each other, but he still steps too close for her comfort.

"Eddie's pretty far away. Wouldn't you rather be with someone closer to home?"

There's no one she'd rather be with.

And Puppyface must still not realize Eddie's planning to come back for good. Interesting.

"This really isn't your business," she tells him in her sternest voice. "And you're harassing me. Go. Away."

"I'm not harassing you. I'm showing *an interest*."

"You're a pig. Your *interest* is not returned."

She tries to step around him but he blocks her path. "Come on, Rocky. Give me a chance. I'm a lot more fun than you give me credit for."

There are plenty of people still milling around, despite the first big exodus as soon as the last bell rang. And she doesn't recognize anyone she could walk toward and talk to.

Because she's relied for so long on her friendship with Anabelle that she doesn't have anyone else. After it was so hard to cultivate new friends in high school, she just...gave up. Put all her social eggs into the proverbial Anabelle-and-Eddie basket, and now...what?

"Let me walk you home." Puppyface moves alongside her and makes to put his arm around her shoulders, and that's the last straw.

"Touch me and regret it."

He grins like a damn psychopath. "What will you do to me?"

She just moves out of his way and keeps walking. If she does anything, she will try to hurt him, and then she'll be the one guilty of assault. Not a good look, and a disciplinary infraction isn't going to serve her well in literally any area of her life. So she walks toward a large cluster of field hockey students getting ready to board one of the team buses, tries to lose him by slipping through their crowd quickly. As a girl, it's easier for her to mix in with the female athletes and get out the other side. Puppyface will be stopped.

And he is. As Raqia walks away, she hears one of the coaches say to him, "Luke, shouldn't you be dressing out for football practice? Get to the boys' locker room, now." And when she glances back over her shoulder, he is indeed heading for the gym.

But his gaze is trained on Raqia, and nothing in his expression makes her think for a moment that she's really gotten away.

When she gets home, Taita is making dinner already, because her friends—the Lebanese Old Ladies Club, as Raqia and Anabelle used to privately call them—are coming over. It's Taita's night to host dinner and canasta. Raqia comes into the kitchen to kiss her hello.

"How was school today, habibti?"

Too much to go into now. "It was okay." She picks up a cut triangle of pita and dips it into the bowl of hummus on a serving tray, then puts it into her mouth so she doesn't have to give her any details.

But Taita's eyes are sharp enough to see what Raqia doesn't want to show her. "I notice you have not been on the phone with Eddie as much this week." She continues slicing cucumbers for salad.

"I've been busy with schoolwork."

"Making time for your studies is important." She puts all the slices into the large wooden salad bowl. "What else is going on?"

Raqia wants to tell her; she did promise to be more open with her grandmother. But telling Taita that she's broken up with Eddie makes it feel too real when Raqia isn't sure she can stay broken up. That just feels like one more bad decision, frankly. Did she really need to let go of him just to handle all of this other stuff? It's not like he's here, anyway. That buzzing wasplike feeling in her stomach is starting to become too familiar.

"Have you talked with Anabelle today?" Taita asks.

"Why? Did she call you again at lunch or something?" God, what else?

"No, no, nothing like that. I have been hoping you would have made up with her by now."

Seriously? "Yeah, me too." She never did get a response from Anabelle to her texts explaining everything. She assumes she's not going to.

Taita stops slicing tomatoes and looks at Raqia with an exasperated expression. "Could you not start the conversation?"

"I tried, Taita, I really did. She's just not ready to talk to me, I guess."

Taita just clucks her disappointment under her breath, mutters a phrase in Arabic Raqia doesn't know.

Raqia chokes down the last of her pita. It feels like she's wrecked every important relationship in her life. "I'm really sorry."

"Ah, well." Taita resumes slicing the ingredients for the salad. "The two of you have strayed far afield from each other, but perhaps things will turn around." But she doesn't look up, the sadness evident on her face. Raqia picks up her backpack and heads down the hall.

"Dinner is at five-thirty," Taita calls after her.

"I'm not hungry," Raqia says before closing herself up in her bedroom.

She dives into her homework; she's almost caught her grades back up to where they were before homecoming. She wants to get even farther, though, to make up for her setbacks and put herself ahead.

About an hour later her phone rings. It's Eddie. She puts her math book aside and picks up the call.

"Hey," she says.

"Hi, Rocky." His familiar baritone is comforting. She curls up onto the pillows of her bed and cradles the phone. "Thanks for letting me call you tonight."

"I'm glad you did." She can't help smiling.

"You...want to tell me about your day?" he asks.

She does, she really does. But there's not much to tell that won't make it seem like she's just complaining about his friends. "It was okay, not awesome, not the worst."

"Yeah." His voice is quiet. They don't say anything for a bit.

"How's your week going?" she asks.

"Marking time, mostly. Our team is traveling this weekend. We have an away game in Louisiana."

"That's great." Then she can't help herself. "You should call Kirstin and tell her about it." Jealousy simmers just under her skin like a poison. "She and Julie were curious about your schedule today at lunch."

Eddie scoffs. "I'm not going to do that. I don't even know how to get in touch with her."

"I'm sure you could get her number from one of your fanboys."

Eddie pauses, then says, "Can we please switch to video? I desperately want to see you."

Raqia's pulse quickens. "Okay," she says, trying to sound even. They switch over, and when his face comes into view, she can't help but smile. "Hey."

He smiles back. "Hey." He pushes his dark hair back from his eyes; even on her tiny screen she can see them brighten while he looks at her. He's settled onto the pillows of his bed, just like she is in her own room. "Rocky, I'm going to tell you something, and I need you to really listen."

Giant moths are divebombing her insides. "I'm listening."

"Good. I don't care if Kirstin or any other girl knows my game schedule. I don't care if Kirstin or any other girl knows *any part* of my schedule. Dinosaurs will roam the earth again before they matter to me. Am I clear?"

Those giant moths transform into butterflies, bright and blue and lovely. "Clear as a jellyfish."

He smiles again. "I'm glad. Now, really pay attention to this second part: the only girl I care about is you."

She closes her eyes, takes a deep breath. "It's really difficult to stay broken up with you when you say things like that."

"Excellent. I have no wish to stay broken up."

"Eddie—"

"Rocky, please. I'm trying to give you the time you need, but I don't really understand what you need it for, and my mind is going in a thousand terrifying directions. Please tell me what's going on."

I'm behind in school. I'm still fighting with your sister. Even Taita thinks I've screwed up, and I haven't talked to my father in three months. I have no other friends. And these animal instincts are too wild for me to keep up with them. I've never been violent before and all I can think about when I see Puppyface is flaying the skin from his body.

Can he withstand the litany of all of that?

"There's a lot," she says instead.

He puts one arm behind his head and seems to settle in even deeper. "I have plenty of time."

She's really tempted. Talking to him might make her feel better, but unloading all of that on him might also convince him she's too much work. She doesn't want to seem difficult; she never has, not to anyone. She's not used to complaining and doesn't want to start now, not with him.

"It's nothing I can't handle," she says quietly.

He's quiet, thoughtful for a long pause. Then finally, "I hope you'll learn you can trust me with it, Raqia. Whatever it is. No matter what direction our relationship takes, be it friendship or more or both, we have a long history together, and I'm not going away."

Tears prick up behind her eyes and she blinks fast to quell them. "I appreciate that," she whispers, and he hears it.

"Enough to let me in on it?" His voice is gentle, hopeful. Tense.

It's tempting, but...not yet. She shrugs. "It's just day-to-day stuff. Nothing exciting."

He considers her face, and she molds her expression into something cheerful. From the thin set of his mouth, she doubts it's fooling him.

After a moment he asks, "What would you like to talk about?"

She clears her throat. "Um, how is football going?"

His eyes darken. "Football? Really?" His voice has gone low. "Do you really want to hear about that?" He shakes his head. "You know, Rocky, one of the things I've always loved about being at your house is that no one there ever asks me about *football*."

She stills. Feels cold all of a sudden.

"In fact, your house might be the only place where who I am isn't reduced to a dog chasing a ball."

"I'm sorry—"

"Why? If you're genuinely interested in the sport that has given me more opportunities than I deserve, I'm happy to talk to you about it. The fact is, football is the one socially acceptable avenue for wolfish violence. It's *celebrated* there, and I hate that. I also love it, because that outlet serves me well, and I can't stand that, either. And it makes me both grateful and furious at the same time that I now have to depend on football for my education, and the more aggressive I am, the more 'alpha'—" He makes annoyed air quotes with two fingers. "Well, the better off I am. But that's really, really *not* who I want to be."

He sighs. There's a sadness in his eyes, but he gives her a wan smile. "So that's how football is going, if you really want to know. But if you're just making conversation for the sake of conversation, let's talk about anything else. Because you're different. And I need that. I crave it."

Raqia doesn't realize her tears have leaked out until one of them drops off her cheek onto her neck. She hastily wipes it away.

Eddie's voice and eyes are so gentle. "I didn't mean to make you cry."

"I just...wish things were easier. I wish...you were here." Admitting it to him out loud loosens something tight in her chest.

He gives her a sweet smile. "I will be, soon."

"Thanksgiving is a long way off."

He laughs gently. "Good news, then. I'll be home the weekend after this one."

"Wait, really?" She sits up. "How?"

"The team we were supposed to play had to forfeit and there wasn't time to schedule another game with someone else. I have the weekend off and I'm coming home."

She really could fly.

"When I get there, can I see you?"

She nods her head vigorously. "I'll clear my calendar."

He laughs at her joke and that makes her laugh. "Good."

Then there's a knock on her bedroom door. Taita calls, "Habibti, you have not eaten yet. Come and get some dinner."

Eddie narrows his eyes at her in mock admonishment. "You need to eat, Rocky. Especially if it's grapeleaves. You need to eat some for me."

She laughs again. "Hang on." She gets up to open the door for Taita, her phone still in hand. "Can I get a plate and eat in here?"

Taita peers at the phone. "Is that Eddie?" She smiles.

"Hi, Taita," he calls. "How are you?" Raqia holds the phone up so her grandmother can talk to him.

"Very good, Eddie. How are you?"

"Missing the best food in the world. And also your granddaughter."

Taita gasps and wags her finger at the screen. "So bold, Eddie." But she doesn't look upset—or surprised. To Raqia she says, "Yes, get a plate and you can eat in your room if you are still talking to Eddie. But if not, you have to come out and visit with our friends."

Raqia nods and closes the door again as her grandmother leaves.

"You have friends over?" Eddie asks.

"*Taita* has friends over. It's the Lebanese Old Ladies Club."

"Ah. Give them all my best." Then he sits up. "In fact, you go get a plate, and I'll make myself a sandwich, and then we can have dinner together, here on the phone."

Raqia nods, giddy, and goes to make a plate. Maybe it's because he's older, maybe it's because he has worked hard to convince people he's not Big Bad material, maybe it's because he's just nice, but she's impressed by how sweet his idea is.

But honestly? She isn't sure she deserves him.

22

T HAT WEEKEND RAQIA APPLIES for several internships she learned about through the counselors' office to the soundtrack of Anabelle and some of her new friends playing frisbee in the Fosters' front yard. If only their backyard hadn't been overtaken by that enormous magnolia tree, they could have hung out back there instead.

Thinking of the magnolia tree reminds her of Eddie and that beautiful flower he gave her the night of the homecoming dance. She left it at Anabelle's house that night, thinking she would retrieve it after the dance, but she never got the chance to. She imagines the petals have probably curled inward like the legs of a dead spider, assuming Anabelle hasn't thrown it away by now. She probably has. She's probably tossed hers out, too. Maybe even stomped on them first.

She peeks out the window and sees Anabelle and the others sitting on the grass, lounging in the shade of a crepe myrtle that towers over their next-door neighbor's house. Chuy reclines in the middle of their gaggle, petted and cooed over by Probably-Ramona. Well, at least he didn't suffer any long-term damage from Raqia's overenthusiastic—oh, fine, call it what it is, *livid and hurt and betrayed*—embrace. So that's good.

Then Anabelle looks up and glances across the street to Raqia's house, sees her in the window looking out at them, and their eyes lock for just a second. Raqia tries to hold her gaze, even gives her a tiny wave. Anabelle doesn't wave back, but she looks thoughtful and gives Raqia a little chin tilt.

That counts as a greeting, doesn't it?

Raqia picks up her phone to text Eddie to ask what he thinks, but stops herself. Their phone conversation Thursday night felt so good. She wants him back.

But she also really wants to handle her problems on her own. To show that she can. He's not going to come in and solve anything for her with Anabelle or her classes or Taita or her father. She doesn't want to lay those problems at his feet, anyway.

So she comes back to her laptop, back to filling out applications. There are two summer internships at the zoo, which would be fun and interesting, but really hot. Houston in the summer really should have a giant air-conditioned dome over the whole city. Even desert animal affinities can't stand the outdoors in July and August in this paved-over swamp. There's another internship at one of the art museums, which would be cool (both figuratively and literally) but very isolated, working with a curator in their archives. And that won't get her any closer to having an advantage applying to Affinity Behavioral Studies programs.

At the back of her desk drawer is the folded-up brochure her doctor gave her, the one about Dr. Delacoeur's study. Maybe it's worth looking into. She reads the brochure again, finds the website, looks it over once more, and applies. Maybe she won't even get in. Best-case scenario, she'll get into all of these and then have her pick. She laughs at herself for even thinking that'll happen. But she's finished another item off her to-do list.

The next day, when Raqia gets to math class right before lunch, she takes her usual spot next to Anabelle, who seems to be trying to finish her homework from the night before, and says hi.

Anabelle doesn't look up from her hastily scribbled matrix calculations but still speaks: "Hello." She begins another problem hesitantly, her long blonde hair falling over their table as she copies it out, then halts.

"Do you want any help?" Raqia asks quietly. "I already did the problem set." She did it last week when she was working on getting ahead. It wasn't hard to teach it to herself from the textbook, but Anabelle has been struggling with this chapter.

"Um…yeah." Anabelle sighs, tossing her pencil down. "I'm not getting it." She angles her body slightly toward Raqia. "I don't want to turn in another late assignment for this class."

Raqia can work with that. As she explains the basic logic behind matrices, Anabelle doesn't make eye contact but nods her head, asks the occasional question, and seems to be understanding her homework problems better. It feels like a thaw.

"Thanks," Anabelle murmurs as their teacher walks in. The bell rings and she quickly finishes up the problem they've been working on together, and the time for conversation is over.

As the teacher begins working out the next concept on the board, it's clear some of the other students are still having trouble with it, even though Raqia isn't. When she's the only one to answer a question correctly, Probably-Ramona mutters something to the person next to her and then they both gigglesnort. Raqia looks back at her and Probably-Ramona's sneer makes it obvious her snide remark was about her. That old feeling of inadequacy, mingled with her wolfish temper, creates nothing good.

She begins the calming breaths Eddie taught her, as quietly as possible, and doodles shrinking spirals in the margins of her notebook to spin the anger down.

Anabelle seems to notice all of it.

Halfway through class, Anabelle slides a scrap of paper over that says only, "Thanks for your texts."

Raqia looks up at her and gets a curt nod in response. She puts the note inside her textbook and feels marginally hopeful.

At the end of class, Anabelle mutters a quick "see you later" but then walks out with Probably-Ramona while Raqia is still packing up her books.

Two steps forward, one step back is still forward progress.

The next night, Raqia sends Eddie a text with a short video of some husky puppies climbing all over each other, yipping and nipping, with the caption **fanboys**. She hopes he finds it funny.

He texts back: **that could be us**

With a wink/kiss emoji.

He doesn't give up. It makes her smile. She holds off for a whole five minutes before calling him. He answers before the first ring has even finished and turns on his video. They catch up about their weekends, their days, for twenty minutes before the conversation navigates to Anabelle.

Eddie fills in the sister-shaped gaps Raqia can't see, from what Anabelle has shared with their mom and that their mom has shared with Eddie.

"And even though you're not hanging out together outside of the classes you share," he says, "there's no longer any mention of animosity toward you. I hope that helps a little."

"I guess it does." Raqia tries not to take it so hard that Anabelle has replaced her with other people who have embraced her in such an immersive way.

"It's a little weird, not gonna lie," Eddie continues. "She's even spending Sundays with the Pippers now." *Pippers* is what some of the affined students at school call the Plain Isn't Pain—or, PIP—clubbers. "I never thought anything would make her abandon going to church, but here we are in a strange new world."

"Yeah, she really seemed all in," Raqia says. But given that Anabelle was always searching for a group to be a part of, maybe this shouldn't be a surprise. After a pause, she asks, "How's Chuy?" She's avoided mentioning the cat, not wanting to bring up what she still thinks of as her disastrous emergence, but the fact is that she actually liked him well enough before all of this started. And as it's almost impossible to separate the idea of Chuy from the idea of Anabelle, asking about him gives her the illusion of *not* asking about Anabelle, even though the whole conversation right now has become about her.

"Chuy's fine," Eddie assures her. "No damage done. Though honestly, nothing you did to that cat compares with the trauma of Anabelle's aggressive affection toward it."

Raqia is quiet before asking, "Do you think Anabelle will get an affinity?" *And if she does, do you think she'll be my friend again?* And would Raqia even want her back at this point?

The dull ache in her chest confirms, yes, she would.

"You know I can't predict that, Rocky." Eddie's quiet but not annoyed. A little tired, maybe. "I'm not worried about it, though; she's barely seventeen. I mean, if she gets all the way through college and doesn't show any evidence of an affinity, then we can start to wonder if she's really Plain."

"I guess so." Raqia has had to shift her thinking about affinities and their capricious timelines ever since hers emerged. It never occurred to her that she would get one before Anabelle, nor that her best friend would lose her ever-loving mind over it.

"Just look at that counselor she's seeing, Ms. Elsa," he continues. "Wasn't she in her late thirties before she turned into, what, a fish?"

"Mermaid, I think. That's what it sounded like."

"Wow, that's wild. Those hybrid affinities are really rare. It doesn't surprise me that hers took so long."

"Maybe Anabelle will be something rare, too." Raqia can hear the wistfulness in her own voice, her deep-rooted hope that Anabelle's wait will have been worth it.

"Maybe." Eddie clears his throat, and when he speaks again, his voice and facial expression are more upbeat. "Let's just...not worry about it, okay?"

"Okay." She can try.

"Let's talk instead about the next time I'm coming home for the weekend."

That sounds good. "Just a few more days, right?" It seems like forever since she saw him.

He grins. "Yep."

She nods. "I know you need to hang out with your fanboys and your family—"

"I do. But you know I'm mostly coming home to see you, right?"

That warm feeling he inspires starts in her belly and radiates everywhere, crescendoing in a blush he can see even on their tiny screens. "Yeah, I guess so..." she teases.

"Come on, Rocky, you know I am." His smile and playful dark eyes tell her he knows this is a game. He knows she's confident in how he feels about her.

She still wants to—needs to—hear him say it.

"You're the reason for everything, Rocky. Always."

And there it is, that tethered feeling she has missed. She used to feel it with Anabelle, too, when they were kids and she thought of her as a sister. She felt it with Taita when she was a child, before she learned to put into words how much she wished her family was more than just one person two generations older. But with Eddie, it's different. With him, she feels less like an accessory, even a loved accessory, to someone else's life; with him, there's an intertwining. Like he's always been there, just waiting for her, wanting her, not out of obligation or because of her dependence on him.

She's going to take him back. She doesn't want to say it yet, but she can feel the inevitability of it, and it fills her with calm.

"I miss you," she says so quietly, he wouldn't be able to hear her without his keener senses.

He smiles at her. "Good," he says softly. "I promise never to take that for granted."

She nods. It's the closest they've ever come to saying they love each other.

Later, when Raqia is trying to fall asleep, she thinks about whether she would sacrifice getting back together with Eddie for her long-time friendship with Anabelle, should it come to that. What she might have with Eddie is so new, still somewhat untested. They've hardly seen each other, as boyfriend and girlfriend, since all of this started.

And she has so many years of friendship with Anabelle—although the last few have felt, if she's being honest, somewhat strained and desperate. A beloved habit, but a habit nonetheless. Their friendship hasn't grown stronger in light of their struggles in high school; it has clung.

And that can't be ignored. It still matters. The ache she feels for that friendship tells her it isn't dead, just...impaired. Undergoing growing pains. She wants to heal it, bring it back.

Anabelle isn't treating her like a best friend by any means, but they still see each other at school. She's not actively hostile anymore and even has short, polite conversations with her now and then. Maybe in time Raqia's being with Eddie will keep her in Anabelle's path enough that the rift between them will patch up. The three of them were a good trio once upon a time. They can be that again, however different it will look. Her call with Eddie that night has her feeling hopeful.

Then Raqia considers that perhaps the home she has always been looking for is the evolving one she already has.

23

A T SCHOOL THE NEXT day, Eddie's fanboys drop in on Raqia during lunch. She's sitting alone, finishing up a lab report for biology that's due by four o'clock while she scarfs down three slices of pizza. Puppyface sits across from her, and then B-Cad and Kiernan slide into the seats on either side of him as if synchronized.

"Hey, Rocky," Puppyface says. There's no hint of levity in the greeting.

"I'd prefer you not call me that," she says, wiping her fingertips on a napkin. "If you're still having trouble pronouncing my name after all this time, it's RAH-kee-uh. Not that hard, just like it's spelled." She goes back to typing up her notes.

There's a void between the three guys, a stillness that she refuses to look at. Maybe Puppyface isn't used to being dismissed publicly. Well, he probably ought to get used to it.

Kiernan clears his throat. "So, *Raqia*, we heard Eddie's coming home this weekend. You know about that?"

"You mean you don't?" Too late she realizes maybe he didn't want them to know for a reason. But last night, he agreed he would need to see them while he was in town. She keeps typing her report to avoid making eye contact and giving anything away.

"How long's he staying for?" Puppyface asks after another quiet minute goes by.

Raqia sighs. She's tired of these boys invading her work table. They're not interested in sitting with her. They're not interested in socializing. They just want information from her about their hero. "A weekend is usually a couple of days, isn't it?"

She moves her fingers just in time before Puppyface slams the lid down on her laptop.

"*What* is wrong with you?" she growls at him.

B-Cad grins. "Aw, there's that cute little wolf."

"Go to hell, Bradford." She piles up her papers and laptop, but before she can stand all the way up, Puppyface has put a strong hand on her wrist, the tips of his claws grazing the tender skin on the inside of her arm. B-Cad and Kiernan tense, but whether to restrain Puppyface or her, she isn't sure. "Let go of me now," she demands, keeping her volume low. The last thing she wants is to be the center of a lunchroom brawl.

"Just tell us."

"Ask him yourself, Puppyface."

The dark fire in his eyes makes it clear he doesn't like her nickname for him. A low growl rumbles out of his chest. She refuses to sit back down.

"Come on, Luke," B-Cad says quietly. "Let her go."

"No, I want to know whether it's true that Eddie is coming back to stay."

Raqia doesn't know how many people he's told about his transfer plans. She hasn't said anything to anyone, and she thought he was going to use this weekend to talk to his parents about it. But maybe some of his teammates know? Maybe the coach had to send another recommendation letter for him and let it slip? Whatever the case, she doesn't want to possibly worsen it by saying anything to these mongrels.

"And I said you should ask *him*." She yanks her wrist out of his grip, but not without incurring some shallow scratch marks. She looks at the thin perforations of blood on her skin, feels the sting of it.

Kiernan whistles low. "Wow. Eddie is really going to hate that."

Raqia glares at him. "*I'm* not a fan, either." She just stops herself from dumping her greasy pizza in Puppyface's lap. It would be childish. And probably provoke a worse response from him, which she really doesn't want to be on the receiving end of. So she gathers everything up, tosses the rest of her lunch, and stalks out of the cafeteria to go to the nurse. Better not to take any chances with whatever bacteria are underneath that jackass's fingernails.

She stops short at the doorway into the hall when she sees Anabelle there with Taylor and yet another girl she's been hanging out with instead of Raqia. Anabelle stares at her then looks back at the table where Puppyface and his friends still are. Puppyface looks *pissed* and is glaring at Raqia. An angry shudder skitters down her spine.

"Are you okay?" Anabelle asks her. She looks...actually concerned. A small, hopeful tremor passes through Raqia at that point. Anabelle gestures with her chin to Puppyface. "That wolf looks like he wants to kill you." She reaches out and touches Raqia's arm, gently turns it over. She tosses two long blonde braids over her shoulders and takes a deep breath. "I think this qualifies as an attack."

The whole scene reminds Raqia briefly of the day they met, the scraped knee on the driveway and her new neighbors rushing outside to see what the commotion was about. Deciding then and there to be her friends, as if it were the easiest and most natural thing in the world. And it was, for so long.

Resentment boils up inside of her—a mood swing that's rapidly becoming familiar, unfortunately. Anabelle looks like she cares, and how much can Raqia trust that now? She really wants to, and Anabelle really looks like she means it.

Taylor and the other girl step away from them, start making small talk. To give them some privacy, perhaps? They have to recognize this longstanding friendship is now in tatters. But a sudden conversation in a crowded hallway isn't going to solve anything, and Raqia has a more pressing concern right now.

"I need to get to the nurse," she says curtly, drawing her arm back out of Anabelle's fingers.

"Um...okay, yeah, of course." Anabelle steps back. "Maybe later we can—"

Raqia stiffens, turns around. "Maybe we can *what*." It's not a question. She wants to both yell at Anabelle and hug her, wants to curse her out and also cry. Her emotions are a soup about to boil over. Because if Anabelle's next words aren't *talk and work all of this out because I miss you,* Raqia might lash out in ways that would not only decimate everything they've ever shared, but also damage her nascent relationship with Eddie. She has to dance carefully on the edge of this claw.

Anabelle looks actually a little bit unnerved.

Good. And Raqia kind of hates herself for thinking so.

"I have to get to the nurse," she says again and walks away without another word or glance back.

24

A COMMUNITY SERVICE EVENT is happening after school on Thursday.

Raqia was sitting in a study carrel across from the school office that morning when she saw Anabelle come out of the conference room with Ms. Elsa. They both looked happy, and Anabelle immediately signed up on a list posted on the bulletin board on the neighboring wall. Raqia went up to investigate and saw that Ms. Elsa had agreed to take a group of students to a block walk for a candidate arguing for Plain rights. Anabelle and Taylor had both signed up.

Raqia added her name, too, then texted Taita to say she'd be home late for a school project but to give the Lebanese Old Ladies Club her love. She tried to sit near Anabelle on the bus heading to the event, but a head nod and a polite smile in acknowledgement of her presence was the best she could get.

Now, at the candidate's campaign headquarters, Raqia and Anabelle, with Taylor and half the Pippers in between them, are listening to their marching orders.

"You don't need to knock on anyone's door," Ms. Elsa is saying. "You don't need to talk to anyone who doesn't talk to you first. Then you're welcome to say what our candidate stands for, but mostly you just want to remind them to exercise their civic duty to vote."

It's very nonconfrontational. All they have to do is leave information cards on the front doors of houses, to remind people to head to the polls on Election Day.

Apparently there are some candidates who think Plain Ones shouldn't be allowed to vote. That seems radically unfair. Even if that's not going to matter to Raqia, who has her affinity now, it *will* matter to Anabelle if she doesn't get one in the next year. And to almost every one of the other students now standing here. Raqia shudders.

"We really appreciate your taking time this afternoon to help out," Ms. Elsa continues. "You'll all get credit for your community service requirement for your civics classes; I'll turn in the list to your principal tomorrow. Be sure to come back here to headquarters, after you've finished your lists, to sign out." As the students begin to disperse, she reminds them all, "Take a buddy! No one goes out there solo."

Anabelle and Taylor head off together, as do the rest of the paired-up students. Raqia is the odd person out and she tries not to let that old fear of rejection bubble up inside of her. She turns around to see if Anabelle and Taylor might still be in sight to try and tag along with them, but they—and everyone else—have already gone.

"Do you need a partner, Raqia?" Ms. Elsa asks.

"You remember my name?" She didn't expect that.

Ms. Elsa tilts her head from side to side. "You and Anabelle made a strong impression on me when we met."

Raqia turns red. "Sorry about that."

She waves her hand dismissively. "Don't be. I know you and Anabelle have been going through some stuff." Then she looks around. "Do you need a walking buddy?"

Raqia nods her head. "Looks like it." She shrugs. "Unless there's something I can help out with here?" She gestures to the office around them. It's quietly busy. No one appears to be frantic or hurried.

Ms. Elsa picks up a stack of door hangers and a clipboard with a list and a pen attached. "I'll walk with you," she says. "We can hit up a couple of the streets in the neighborhood behind the headquarters."

"Are you sure?" Raqia asks, remembering their first meeting, when Ms. Elsa recoiled slightly upon learning she was a wolf. Maybe Ms. Elsa doesn't really want to be around her and is just being polite.

"Of course."

So they go.

While they walk, adding a door hanger at each of the houses on their list, Raqia wonders how much Anabelle has told her about what's been happening between them. Or if Anabelle mentions her at all.

"So how have things been going?" Ms. Elsa asks.

"I mean, okay, I guess." She doesn't know how much she wants to reveal. "I've been applying for summer internships. Hopefully I'll get a good one that will make my college applications look better."

"Do you know yet what you want to study?"

Raqia nods. "Affinity Behavioralism."

"That sounds really interesting!" Ms. Elsa seems very encouraging. Maybe it's genuine? "There are some really good programs in Texas. A&M has one, and I think the University of Houston has a program that conjuncts with the zoo here."

"I've heard that."

"Or would you like to go far away for college?" She hands Raqia another short stack of door hangers as they walk up to the next house.

"I hadn't really considered that." She doesn't want to leave Taita all alone here. And now Eddie is coming back for good—maybe a little bit, in part, for her. Of course, they could always go somewhere else together.

Seriously, settle down, she chastises herself. *Don't get so far ahead of yourself. You don't even know if this thing with him is going to work out.*

But if she's being honest with herself, she really hopes it does.

They're moving through their house list quickly. In fifteen minutes, they're halfway done.

"Is this all we have to do?" Raqia asks. "Just put these flyers on people's doors?"

"There are all kinds of things people can do to help out," Ms. Elsa says. "I like volunteering. It's a big part of what we do at Phoenix Group."

"Can you...can you tell me more about what they do?"

"Sure. Outreach looks like a lot of different things. Political action, lobbying. Our board president testified on Capitol Hill last year to talk about

Plain Ones' rights. Sometimes we have specialists who investigate unusual affinities."

"You mean like when someone claims to be a phoenix?"

Ms. Elsa nods. "Yes, but also rare hybrid affinities, like mine. For example, my cousin's next-door neighbor has a son who's a centaur. He'll probably become a movie star. A lot of hybrids go into the entertainment industry."

Raqia thinks of Alain's friend. "One of our classmates is a manticore. He'll probably never become famous for anything good. He's a total d-bag."

Ms. Elsa laughs at that; the sound puts Raqia more at ease. "It happens. Our group also does counseling, like I'm contracted to do at your school."

"Are you going to be here permanently?"

Ms. Elsa smiles. "Just this semester." She marks a few other houses off their list.

"So why do you do it?" Raqia gestures toward Ms. Elsa's whole person: thick hair, pretty eyes, hourglass shape. "I mean, you could probably be a celebrity."

"Oh, thank you for that, but I don't know if I could." She shrugs. "I'd rather be doing this anyway. It feels meaningful. I was a Plain One for so long, and it was a difficult life. I don't want other people to have to go through what I did. I can't ever forget that having an affinity is a privilege, and if I can use mine to help other people, then I will."

That...sounds like Eddie. Putting aside the easy and popular thing, the thing that makes his father proud, so he can do something useful with his life and help the people around him.

Ms. Elsa hands Raqia the last of the door hangers. "We're almost done! I appreciate your helping out today."

"It feels like the least amount of effort someone could give to a cause and still participate."

And Raqia wants to participate. Eddie's example has inspired her. If he can use his influence to shepherd his fanboys into good behavior, she can use her privilege to make the world safer for people who are Plain.

"Can I ask you something personal?" Raqia says as they walk back.

A beat of hesitation, then: "I suppose so."

"When Anabelle first told you I was a wolf, you seemed...I don't know, nervous."

"I'm sorry for that. I shouldn't have made you feel uncomfortable."

"It's okay, I know the news out there is bad. I was just wondering whether...you'd had any bad experiences with wolves yourself." Ms. Elsa stops and looks at her. "I mean, you don't have to answer that if you don't want to." Now Raqia regrets bringing it up. It's too personal, and maybe she doesn't want to know the answer, after all.

"There was a pack starting to organize in the neighborhood I lived in before my affinity emerged. They didn't take kindly to Plain Ones." She doesn't say anything else, and the silence hangs between them like a strung-up deer.

"I'm sorry," Raqia mutters. "But not all wolves are Big Bads."

"Not all wolves," Ms. Elsa agrees. "Yet somehow, whenever there was trouble, it was always a wolf."

Raqia's stomach sinks. There's a lot of prejudice out there. No wonder Eddie works so hard to be everyone's favorite guy. If Eddie can act in ways that prove not all wolves are bad, then she can do that, too—if she can curb the storm that sometimes swirls up inside of her.

"I'd like to change the perception of wolves in the world," Raqia says.

Ms. Elsa gives her a shallow smile. "I'd love that. If there's going to be change, it's going to happen one wolf at a time."

Just like gathering the votes for her candidate: one person at a time. It's a slow way to make change. Maybe Dr. Delacoeur's study will lead to faster results.

They get back to the candidate's headquarters just as most of the other students are returning, Anabelle and Taylor included. Raqia notices they're holding hands when they walk up to the building and smiles to herself. Soon everyone has signed out and is filing back onto the bus to go back to school. Raqia doesn't try to sit near them, gives them space.

Later, as Raqia is walking home, she gets a text...from Anabelle.

thanks for coming to the block walk

Raqia smiles. **sure, it was a good thing to do**

but you're not even Plain

that doesn't mean I don't care

There's an empty silence for another minute before Anabelle texts again:

anyway, thank you

Raqia feels lighter than she has in a while. She smiles as she texts her back:

you're welcome

A minute later, she sends Anabelle another text: **do you want to maybe hang out this weekend?** Eddie is going to be home. It'll be an easy opportunity—

I can't.

already have plans?

Anabelle doesn't answer. Oh. Well, it was worth a shot. Maybe it's still too soon. Some of the buoyancy Raqia has been feeling the last few minutes deflates.

But still, it's better than nothing.

25

When Raqia gets home from school on Friday afternoon, her grandmother isn't alone. Raqia hears the friendly chatting and laughter from the driveway, and when she comes through the front door, there's Eddie, sitting at the kitchen table with Taita while she rolls raw pita dough into balls and places them between two clean cotton tablecloths for their second rising. Raqia drops her backpack by the couch in the living room.

"Ah, there you are, habibti!" Taita says with a smile. "Eddie came home early from school and marched himself right over here to visit with me."

"How nice of him," Raqia says, giving her grandmother a kiss hello on her cheek. "And shrewd," she continues, giving him a sly side-eye.

"I'm no dummy," he says cheerfully, resting his elbow on the table and his chin on his hand. But there's a shameless hunger in his eyes, too. They follow Raqia around the room as she washes her hands, dries them, pours herself a small glass of milk. She can't help looking back at him every few seconds, but then she has to turn away each time or she'll turn bright red in front of Taita. She stands at the counter to drink, hoping the frigid milk will cool her off. It doesn't.

When she puts her glass in the sink, she says, "It certainly got quiet in here all of a sudden. I could hear you two having a great time from outside."

"Eddie is so entertaining," Taita says. "He was telling me all about school."

"Really?" Raqia asks. The wolf in question is still gazing at her. Raqia would call his expression heart-eyes if he didn't look, frankly, a little dangerous.

And frankly—surprisingly—she likes it.

"Yes, yes," Taita sighs. She rolls the last bit of pita dough, tucks it into a ball, and places it beneath the top tablecloth. She stands and lifts the large metal bowl from the table and brings it to the sink, washes it out.

"How long do these have to rise, Taita?" Eddie asks. He sits up straight but is still looking at Raqia.

She lifts her eyebrows at him as she dries her hands. "You suddenly have an interest in cooking?"

"Homemade pita is the best." He shrugs, grinning. "Might as well learn how to make it myself."

"Oh, of *course*." Raqia laughs. "Because every college student has five hours to spare to bake bread."

"Gotta eat," he says.

Taita chuckles as she puts the cleaned bowl away, then gestures toward the table. "Those will need to rise for another half-hour or so." She places the towel back on the bar handle of the top oven. There are two ovens, which Taita has always insisted is a requirement for a Lebanese woman's kitchen.

"Yes, then comes the laborious process of flouring and rolling out each of those little round puffs of dough," Raqia says. "Then sliding the loaves into the bottom oven to bake, waiting till they inflate, then sliding them out of the bottom oven and into the top one to brown slightly. It takes forever."

"Some things are worth the wait," Eddie murmurs. His focus on Raqia has become intense. Clearly Taita is just ignoring it, because how could she miss the way he's looking at her?

Thoughtful of her, Raqia thinks. She gazes back at Eddie, admires the dark sweep of his hair, his strong arms.

"Well," Taita says, startling Raqia's attention away from him, "I have things to do while we wait for the dough. You two be good." She smiles at them both and heads toward the back of the house.

"We will," Raqia promises.

When Taita is out of earshot, Eddie says, "You didn't kiss *me* hello."

Raqia grins and walks over to him. An electric feeling surges through her. "Are you becoming Lebanese already?" she teases, trying to dispel the nervous energy.

He pulls her quickly onto his lap. "Maybe." He shrugs. "Why not?"

Ha, as if it were so easy to become something else. But Eddie has never needed to become anything other than what he is, has probably never wanted to.

"Kiss me, please," he whispers, his hands resting on her hip, on the small of her back.

She does then, and he returns it hungrily, almost forcefully. She matches his pace, her hands finding his shoulders and clinging there. She has missed him, never wants him to leave again. Most of her other problems seem smaller when she's with him.

She pushes him away after a few minutes, when she hears a conspicuously loud noise coming from the laundry room in the back of the house. Nothing serious, just Taita reminding them she's still here and to behave themselves. He nips gently at her bottom lip.

"I need to get you alone," he murmurs.

"And why is that?" she asks, pretending she doesn't know.

He pulls her closer, tighter. "I've missed you."

And this close to him, she can feel the truth of it. She kisses him again, quickly, draws back as he leans forward, lips parting. She nuzzles her nose against his but withholds her kiss.

"Stop teasing me," he whispers, grinning, but she knows he likes it, too. He loves the pursuit. And if he catches her? Then what?

She gives him free rein for just a few minutes, then pushes slowly away when it sounds like Taita is coming back.

"Rocky, please." His voice is low, his pupils blown wide.

"Shh," she whispers, smiling at him. She stands but he catches one of her hands before she can step away.

He cocks his head, listening as Taita's footsteps come closer, but she goes off into another room before getting to the end of the hallway. Still, with her in the house, it's time to lower the temperature.

"What are your plans this weekend?" Raqia asks.

Eddie shakes his head as if to clear it, then looks up at her. "Spend as much time with you as possible?"

She laughs. "Obviously. What else?"

He sighs, seeming to accept that she wants to have an actual conversation, even if it's only about logistics. His thumb rubs circles on the back of her hand. Every nerve inside her feels ready to pounce.

Focus, she mouths at him.

He grins. *I am.* Says aloud, "I still have to talk to my parents about school. I've been putting it off, and it's not going to be pretty."

"Do you want me there with you?"

"More than anything," he says, "but I have to do it alone." Then he shakes his head again, resigned. "I don't think you'll want to be there anyway. Dad's going to be very angry, very growly."

The idea that she can't handle a little growling now is funny to her, but she suppresses it. Eddie is clearly apprehensive.

"Is Anabelle going to be home? Does she know yet?"

"She isn't. I told her, and she didn't really seem surprised."

"I didn't tell her. I didn't tell anyone."

"I know." He smiles softly. "Rocky, she knows about us. She's not...mad about that."

Raqia tries not to pout. "Then what is she still mad about?"

He shrugs. "I think she's just frustrated in general." He squeezes her hand. "I don't think it really even has to do with you in particular."

Then why does it feel like it?

"You know how stubborn she is, how she needs time to figure things out sometimes. Don't underestimate what you've meant to her."

Raqia shakes her head. "It's hard not to when she barely speaks to me."

He lifts her hand to his lips, soothes her with a tender kiss there. "You needed space, didn't you? From me?"

Grudgingly, she nods.

"She needs some, too." He kisses her hand again. "Trust me."

Raqia sighs. "I'll try."

He gives her a pointed look that makes her smile.

"Fine," she relents. "Enough about Anabelle for tonight."

He nods his approval. Cute.

Then he continues, "And tomorrow I'll need to spend some time with the guys," and his expression darkens. Raqia told him about her conversation with Puppyface and the others in the lunchroom. Eddie was pissed at how Puppyface had treated her.

"That sounds like it will take up most of your weekend." He'll probably have to leave right after lunch on Sunday to go back to school.

He stands and pulls her close. "Oh, I want you with me when I see them."

She stiffens in his arms. "Your fanboys? Why would you want me there?"

He looks confused. "Why wouldn't I?"

Taita walks back into the living room then and makes a soft cooing sound. "Eddie, will you have dinner with us?" she asks. She gestures to the kitchen table. "We will have fresh bread."

He smiles. "I would love that, Taita. I don't think my parents will mind, as long as I go spend the rest of the afternoon at home."

"It is settled then. We will see you at seven."

"Yes, ma'am," he answers crisply then kisses them both on the cheek good-bye.

After he leaves, Taita says, "I enjoyed my visit with Eddie."

"Yeah?" Raqia smiles and pours herself another glass of milk. "Same old boy from across the street as always?" *Charming, a little dangerous, kind of makes you worry?*

Taita sighs as she tests the rising dough under the top tablecloth. "No, habibti, he is different. Older, yes, but more...serious also. More...wise."

"Well, I think you lectured him all throughout high school more than his own mother did about making sure he didn't turn out to be a Big Bad." Raqia finishes her milk and washes her hands.

"Oh, I was not *that* strict with him." Taita rolls the tablecloth back. "These are ready, I think."

How strict will you be with him now? Raqia wonders. *How strict will you be with me, about him?* She turns on the ovens, flours the clean countertop, and gets out Taita's wooden rolling pin.

There's just enough time, after they finish baking the bread, for Raqia to rinse off from the heated and floury kitchen and change clothes before Eddie comes back over. She puts on a new pair of fitted jeans and a super-soft top that buttons down the front. Her hair she leaves long, in loose waves.

When she answers the doorbell, Eddie looks glum, staring off into some middle distance between his feet, but he perks up immediately when he sees her.

"You look *very* nice," he says, stepping over the threshold and hugging her. "You smell good, too."

"Thanks." She smiles at him. "So do you."

Taita comes over then and gives Eddie a warm hug. "Dinner is almost ready," she says. "Come in, come in."

While they eat, Eddie gives them what Raqia is sure must be the short version of the last couple of hours.

"I told my parents I wanted to come back to Houston when the term ends next month."

"Do you mean for the holidays?" Taita asks. "Why would you not? Is your family traveling?"

"No, Taita," he says gently. "I want to transfer to a school here. I'm looking at both Rice and U of H."

"Oh," she says softly, glancing at Raqia. "That is a big change."

"It would be," he says. "But the right one."

Taita coos under her breath.

"How did they react?" Raqia asks.

Eddie pauses to eat another bite of warm pita with butter before answering. "About as well as we thought they would." He smiles at Taita. "Dinner is delicious, as always."

"Good, good. But why would they not want you back home?" Perceptive, as always.

"It's complicated, Taita," Raqia says. She's not sure how much Eddie wants to go into detail about it right now.

"Don't worry," he says, "I'm sure it will all work out. I think they're just...shocked by my decision, that's all. It came as a surprise to them." He gives Taita a reassuring shrug. "But would it be okay for me to hang out here for a while after dinner? You know, just till they go to sleep."

Raqia loves this idea. She squeezes his hand under the table; he squeezes back.

Taita gives him a knowing smile. "You fought and do not want to fight again until everyone has slept on it."

He cocks his head at her. "You know me well, Taita."

"Yes, I like to think so."

Raqia says, "We can watch some movies if you want."

"A perfect Friday night," Taita chirps.

After dinner Eddie and Raqia help clean up the kitchen, then they take their bowls of ice cream into the living room to watch *Star Wars*. Taita makes a valiant attempt to watch it with them, but she grows sleepy before half an hour has past and excuses herself.

"You two have fun, and be good. Do not stay too late, Eddie, or your mother might worry."

"I won't, Taita," he promises her.

The thought that Mrs. Foster will be worried about her well-behaved college-age son when she knows he's over here, across the street, is funny to Raqia, but she just wishes her grandmother good-night and settles into the bend of Eddie's arm behind her.

He waits only fifteen minutes after Taita's bedroom door has closed and she has grown quiet before turning the volume on the movie down just a little bit. Then he stands and pulls Raqia up from the couch. "Come with me," he whispers.

Eddie has been in Raqia's bedroom before, of course, when he and Anabelle and Raqia were children. But it's been years, and back then he wasn't holding Raqia's hand, leading her down the hall, or quietly closing the door behind them. Every part of her is silently singing as he sits on the edge of her bed and pulls her close. She stands facing him, arms draped across his shoulders, and dips her head down to kiss him. His hands at her waist gently squeeze, the way they did at the dance that night, when all of this started.

"How long can I stay?" he murmurs.

Taita is a light sleeper and wakes up early and often. If she thinks Eddie has spent the night—or worse, finds him in here—all her good will toward him will be tarnished, perhaps irrevocably.

"Midnight?" That seems like a reasonable curfew, even for Taita.

Eddie pulls Raqia's phone from her back pocket and glances at the time, half past nine. Puts the phone on her nightstand.

"That works," he says.

She rests her forehead against his. "Was your dad really angry?" She keeps her voice quiet.

"I haven't seen him so mad in a long time," he whispers. "He threatened to cut me off entirely if I gave up my scholarship. I said that didn't matter if he wasn't paying for school anyway."

Mr. Foster would *not* have loved that.

Eddie sighs in that sad puppy dog way of his. "So then he said if I don't get my education sorted before the holidays—whatever, wherever it will be—I could consider myself kicked out."

Raqia goes cold. She lifts her head back from him. "Does he not want you to be an engineer?"

"Oh, he thinks that would be fine, if I don't get into the NFL." He rolls his eyes. "It'll be fine." He looks intently at her. "I have a plan. For all of it."

"Okay, that's good, but—"

Then Eddie picks her up, flips their places, and she's lying flat on her back on the bed. She gasps as he hovers over her.

He puts a finger to his lips. "Shh..." A slightly feral smile.

She narrows her eyes and gestures between them. "Surely you don't think we're going to—"

He shakes his head. "Not tonight."

She lets out a breath she didn't know she was holding. "Good. I'm not ready for that."

"I know." He traces a gentle finger down the side of her face. "I'm not yet, either. I don't want to rush that, not with you."

She smiles, pulls him down for a kiss. "Smart boy."

He grins back, moves over so they can be more comfortable. Less tempted. *Maybe.* He stretches out next to her.

"So what is your plan?" she murmurs just as he begins kissing her neck.

He stills. "You really want to know?"

"Of course."

A pause. "Now?"

"Eddie."

"Okay." He props himself up on one elbow. "I should find out about my transfer by the time my current term ends, right before Thanksgiving. It won't be hard to make a decision on which school to go to; that choice will be purely economic. I'm not even going to worry about how much playing time each team will offer me. I don't care."

Raqia isn't sure if he really means that or if it's just a way for him to get back at his dad for being so hung up on this one thing Eddie is good at. But that's not what's most important right now.

"So you won't get kicked out of your house?" Raqia doesn't think Taita would let him stay here if he did, and she might even decree they couldn't date: her worries would be too amplified. Raqia reaches for Eddie's hand, and he clasps hers back. They'd find a way.

He gives her a little smile. "I don't think that's a real threat, no." Then he kisses her. "It's sweet of you to worry about it, but don't."

"I'll make an effort. Now what about your fanboys?"

"Whatever. If they really were my 'fanboys,' as you and my sister insist on calling them, they'd be easier to manage."

"I know they're forming a pack around you. I mean, anyone with eyes and two brain cells to rub together can see it."

"Yeah." His sigh sounds weary. And a little wary. "I didn't ask for that—"

She pushes him, playfully. "Don't even *try* to pretend you don't like it."

"Oh, really?" He tickles her side and she has to stifle her laugh. "Shh, Rocky, we have to be quiet." Tickles her some more. Hovers over her again. "I can't help it if some of those guys need a more dominant wolf to teach them how to behave." Then his gaze turns more serious. "I was actually hoping you would...well. Join us."

She stares at him. "Join your fledgling pack?" It isn't the community she was looking for, but it would mean social bonds. New friends, and more than just Puppyface. The other guys. Maybe their girlfriends, if Kirstin and Julie can be nice to her. Probably others, as time goes on. She can work with that.

She wouldn't be alone.

"Yes. Please." He kisses her again. "You're one of us, Rocky."

She grins. "Are you saying I need a 'more dominant wolf,' too?"

He grins and gestures around them. "Only in here." He goes back to nuzzling her neck. His warm breath on her skin makes her shiver. She pushes him gently away. He says, "In all seriousness, Rocky, you would be...my equal. Help me...I don't know, lead them."

She stares at him. "You really think I could?"

He nods. "I'm so much better when I'm with you. I'm calmer. Stronger. Everything just feels better."

Something warm and sweet blooms inside of her, like a kaleidoscope of mandalas. "I get that," she whispers. When she's with him, her craze of emotions feels contained, like he can hold all of it in. Even at her most feral, like that night in the movie theater, with Eddie she can feel wild and calm at the same time. It doesn't make logical sense in her mind, but it does in her core, in her cells. "You make me feel...safe." She lightly drags her fingertips up and down his arms.

"Will you, then?" His voice is even, but his eyes are dark and a little wild, and his arms are clearly straining to keep himself off of her.

She smiles at him and pulls him closer. "I can try."

Oh, his mischievous grin. *"Excellent."*

26

E ARLY ON SATURDAY AFTERNOON, Raqia goes over to Eddie's. Anabelle is out, unfortunately; she's gone to the mall with Taylor. That's nice for her, at least.

Raqia and Eddie are going to grab lunch with his fanboys. Or rather, his pack. She has misgivings about calling it that overtly; deep associations with that word prick at her anxiety. It doesn't matter that Eddie wants his pack to be different, a brave new model. Wanting something and enacting it are two different things, and if he's not going to command them by sheer force of will, they have to be prepared that things might not go smoothly.

Especially with Eddie gone at school for another month.

To underscore Raqia's concerns, the first person they see when they head out to the car is Puppyface, sitting casually on the rear bumper of his own car, blocking the Fosters' driveway.

"Hey, Luke," Eddie says as they approach.

"Eddie." He nods. "Raqia." He emphasizes the syllables of her name just slightly. Not enough for Eddie to notice, perhaps, but she hears it, just like she's sure Puppyface means for her to. He gestures to her hair, which she's left long now that the weather has turned cooler. "Very fetching." The smallest of leers on his mouth.

"Where's everyone else?" Eddie asks. "You didn't want to meet at the restaurant?"

"They're coming here. I asked them to show up a few minutes late so I could talk to you first."

Raqia's hackles rise.

"What about?" Eddie asks, his voice casual. But his arm tightens slightly around her waist.

"You need a second, while you're away." It takes Raqia only a moment to realize he means *second-in-command*.

"No. This isn't going to be like that."

"Come on, Eddie," Puppyface says. "You know that's how these things work. The hierarchy matters—"

"Not as much as you think it does. We're not going to be like other packs."

An intense wave of relief washes over Raqia at that. Now they just need Puppyface to not cause trouble.

Eddie continues, "I agreed to organize with all of you because I honestly think there's a benefit to it."

"And because it was happening anyway, whether you wanted it or not."

Eddie shrugs. "I can't deny it. But I'm only participating if it's on my terms."

There's a quiet moment. Raqia is anchored by Eddie's stillness, how he doesn't need to fill the pause with explanation or rationalizing. Puppyface looks around, like he's building up to his next question.

"I hear you're coming back to Houston for good. Is that true?"

Eddie doesn't ask how he knows. "It is. I'll be transferring to a school here."

"Yeah?" Puppyface looks intrigued. "Which one?"

"I haven't decided yet." Eddie shrugs. "I have options."

"How nice."

Raqia asks, "Have you finished your applications yet?" Puppyface is a senior, so he should be most of the way through them by now. "Where are you looking to go?"

Puppyface grins. "Eager for me to stay, little wolf?"

Eddie gives him a warning rumble low in his throat, but Raqia puts a gentle hand on his chest.

Then she turns on her sweetest smile and says, "Not especially, if I'm being honest."

"Aw, don't be that way," he drawls. "Aren't we friends?"

"You cannot be serious."

Before Puppyface can respond, Eddie steps closer to him and says, "If I ever hear that you've threatened Raqia or tried to intimidate her again, you will be out of this pack. Am I clear?" His voice is quiet but stern.

"What, is she telling stories on me now?"

"That implies it isn't the truth," Raqia says, her own voice rising in pitch. She tamps it down. "When you know it is. Can you even *have* a normal conversation with a woman?"

Eddie says, "She didn't have to say anything; I saw the scratch marks on her wrist. *That will not stand.* Harm her, and I will put you in the *hospital*. Am. I. Clear?"

Puppyface exhales sharply through his nose and looks away. "You are."

"I'd like an apology," Raqia says sharply. Eddie steps back and stands next to her. She can feel him slowly calming himself, one barely audible deep breath at a time.

Puppyface glares at her. "An apology? For what?" One side of his mouth tilts up in a smirk. "Showing an interest in Eddie? Or in how you're doing, adjusting to life as the leftover half of the weird sisters?"

"Luke—" Eddie begins but interrupts himself when he sees B-Cad, Mark, and Kiernan walking up to them from a few houses away. They call out their greetings.

"Apologize now," Raqia says, "or do it in front of them. It's up to you."

With angry eyes, Puppyface stands and makes an exaggerated bow, then says in a low voice, "My sincerest regrets, my lady." Then he walks over to greet the other guys with some dopey version of a secret handshake.

"Is he always like that?" Raqia mutters to Eddie.

"Pretty much."

"Why do you put up with him at all?"

"It's better than unleashing him on the rest of the world."

Then the others reach them and there are greetings all around, the usual enthusiasm for Eddie and even genuine friendliness toward Raqia. Puppyface recedes into the background, subdued.

"Hey, Raqia!" B-Cad exudes a retriever-like cheerfulness. "Are you one of us now?"

She smiles in spite of her nervousness. "Looks that way."

"Nice!" He's such a...happy guy. Familiar with people immediately. She's decided to forgive him for his condescending remark in the cafeteria, this time, since he probably didn't intend it that way.

"I'm hungry," Mark says. "Are we going out for pizza, or what?"

"Yeah," Eddie says with a smile and clicks his key fob. "Pick a car and file in."

Lunch goes by largely without incident, though Raqia is surprised by how much these guys can eat. She has three slices, but altogether they consume four large pizzas. She grows more comfortable around them as the hour goes on. Eddie sits as close to her as humanly possible without making things awkward, sometimes intertwining their fingers under the table or resting his hand lightly on her thigh. She doesn't mind that at all. And the other guys are actually...pretty nice, now that they see her as one of them.

Puppyface, though—well, the best she can say about him is that he keeps mostly quiet on one end of the giant booth they're in. He has been chastised, and he's not causing a scene. It's good enough.

She and Eddie drive back to his house alone, and on the way, her phone pings with a bunch of emails. She disengages her hand from his and opens her messages. A tremor, hot and cold, nervous and excited, sweeps through her.

"What's up?" Eddie asks.

"I've been accepted by two internships for this summer." She never thought she'd have a choice, not really. She hoped, but—

"That's great! Which ones?"

"One of the Junior Keeper Programs at the zoo."

He grins. "Probably fun, but hot and smelly."

She scrunches her nose. "Probably."

"And the other?"

She almost doesn't want to tell him; she doesn't know how he'll react. "So...you know that study out of A&M that's happening at the Med Center here?"

His grin fades.

She continues, "Dr. Delacoeur's?"

"You applied for that?"

She nods. "But not as a subject! As a research student."

He shakes his head. "I really don't like the idea of you being anywhere near that study."

"Are you saying I can't do it?"

He glances sharply back at her indignant tone. "Raqia, I would never." He faces forward again. "That's not up to me; it's your decision."

But he doesn't like it.

She says, "I wouldn't have to go to College Station. Dr. Delacoeur has an office here. That's where the internship is."

"That's good." But it's not enough to make him comfortable with it.

She continues, "My doctor thought my perspective would be valuable."

Eddie sighs. "He's right; it will be." He looks over at her. "But *please* be careful, if you pick that one."

"The advantage is that this internship is paid. I think...I'm considering taking it."

He nods. "I get that." When they stop at a red light, he takes her hand and squeezes it. Leans over to give her a small kiss. "I'll worry about you, though. I'm not sure how much I trust that study."

She shudders inwardly. "That's fair. I'll be careful." He nods and turns onto their street. "I don't have to decide today, anyway." But the more she thinks about it, the more she wants to pursue it. Knowing more about how and why the wolves are changing is just too interesting. The science is just too valuable.

When Eddie pulls into his driveway, Anabelle and Taylor are just walking in the front door.

"Oh good," he says, mischief in his eyes. "My sister and the bunny boy."

Raqia puts a hand on his arm. "I need to talk to her. And I need you not to make it worse. His name is Taylor. Be. Nice."

He turns off the car and kisses her tenderly. Winks. "Sure, Rocky. Anything you say."

"I mean it."

He puts a hand over his heart. "You have my word as a wolf."

Great.

When they walk in, Anabelle and Taylor are sitting on one end of the couch in the living room, laughing at a video on his phone. Both of them look up sharply, mirth vanished, when Raqia and Eddie come into the room. Taylor inches away from Anabelle, who just glares at him. He shrugs.

"Hey, sis," Eddie says cheerfully. "Taylor. How's it going?" He plops down in an armchair across from them and half waves in their direction. "As you were."

"What do you want, Eddie?" Anabelle asks, exasperated.

He lifts his hands in a *what??* gesture. "Just hanging out on a Saturday afternoon, home from college. Y'all?"

Raqia, who has been hovering back at the edge of the room, says, "Actually, Anabelle, could I talk to you for a minute, please?"

All of them turn toward Raqia. Eddie gives her an encouraging little smile.

"Um…sure." Anabelle stands up and looks down at Taylor. "You want anything from the kitchen?"

He just shakes his head. It's almost comical how nervous he looks.

"At ease, my dude," Eddie says. "Let's go to the den and give them a few minutes to talk."

"I'm not sure—"

"Taylor," Anabelle says, a little wearily, "my brother is not going to eat you. Go pick out a movie or something. I'll be in there in a few minutes."

The guys head into the den and Raqia follows Anabelle into the kitchen.

"He seems a little skittish," she says.

Anabelle pulls out two dessert plates and forks. "We can't all have big, scary boyfriends."

"About that. Are you going to be okay with me and Eddie? Dating, I mean."

Anabelle exhales heavily. "Yeah."

Raqia wasn't actually expecting that, not without an argument. "Really?"

"Really. I never did have a problem with it. I think you're well-suited. I was just upset at the thought that you'd been hiding it from me. That idea hurt."

"I wasn't hiding anything. I would never do that."

"I know that now. Homecoming weekend was just…a lot of things happened in a short period of time that—" She shrugs. "Between Taylor standing me up and Eddie inviting us to go with him and his friends, it kind of felt like he was maneuvering you to make you his date without telling you. But then I thought that was a really weird thing for him to do and that you must be in on it, and you just didn't want to tell me."

Wow. "That didn't seem a little…contrived to you?"

"I mean, it did." They both laugh a little and it cracks the tension some. Raqia leans on the kitchen island while Anabelle takes a small cardboard box out of the fridge. "But then I was already on edge from the robbery that morning, and then there was that fight at the dance, and then you got sick, and the next day your affinity just burst out right in my bedroom. Eddie and I were already fighting, over you—"

"Wait, why over me?" She can hardly remember everything that happened that night, she was so sick.

"He was upset at how I was treating you. He called me insensitive." She pulls a large knife out of a drawer then looks Raqia in the eye. "I'm sorry for that."

Raqia didn't expect that, either, but she welcomes it. "Thank you."

Anabelle nods. "Anyway, I think it was all just a perfect swarm hitting me that weekend, and I didn't handle it well."

That's an understatement, but Raqia appreciates that Anabelle is telling her all of this. Maybe working with Ms. Elsa has been good for her?

Anabelle opens the box and pulls out a small cake with what looks like cream cheese frosting and orange icing carrots on the top, inexpertly made. She slices into it and puts a piece on each plate.

"Is that...homemade carrot cake?"

"Yeah. I really could've used your superior culinary skills while I was making it, too." She glances toward the den." Do you think he'll like it?"

"Who, Taylor?" It's a little on-the-nose. Raqia grins. "No idea, but even if he doesn't, the fact that you made it for him is *adorable*."

"Don't patronize me," Anabelle mutters, but there's no bite in her tone.

"I'm not." Raqia stifles a laugh. "It's really very sweet of you. He has to like that."

"I'm sure if he doesn't, Eddie will terrorize him until he does."

That idea is so ridiculous they both start giggling. It feels good to share that.

"I'm glad you two are finally getting together," Raqia says.

"Well, it's early still, but I like my chances." Anabelle smiles at her, and Raqia's heart soars.

"We both said some things that weren't nice," Raqia says. "We both acted like... Well, we weren't at our best. Neither of us."

Anabelle nods.

"I'm sorry, too," Raqia says. "I've missed you."

Anabelle smiles. "Same here."

"You know, things don't have to be different between us. I mean, obviously things are different between Eddie and me. But you and me—nothing there has to change." *Please, please agree,* she thinks.

"I like that idea," Anabelle says, leaning on the island, her chin on one hand. "But they are going to change. They *have* changed. And maybe that's okay."

Raqia's nerves go on alert. "What do you mean?"

"This mess has forced us to branch out. Make new friends rather than just rely on each other for everything."

Raqia compares the Pippers to Eddie's pack and their girlfriends, and her chest feels tight. "Somehow I think you're getting the better end of that deal."

Anabelle smiles. "You know, I think my new friends are going to like you, too. Especially when I tell them how great you are."

Raqia thinks about Probably-Ramona. "They don't already dislike me?" She hasn't even bothered to verify the girl's name. It's possible she would be justified in that dislike.

"No one who matters dislikes you."

The tightness in Raqia's chest loosens and she heaves an exaggerated sigh. "I guess I could give them a chance." Then smiles, so Anabelle will know she's kidding.

Anabelle walks around to Raqia's side of the island and hugs her. "We'll still have each other."

Hugging Anabelle after these past awful weeks feels like every last thing becoming right with the world. "That's what I really want."

Anabelle lets go and picks up the cake plates. "Come on, let's go rescue Taylor from the big bad wolf."

They go into the den to find both the guys playing a video game. Taylor doesn't look comfortable, exactly, but he also doesn't look like he's going to pass out from fear, either.

Eddie looks up at Raqia. *All good?* he mouths. She nods, and he smiles.

"Taylor, this has been fun," he says, putting his game controller on the table. "But I'm going to head out." He offers him one of those elaborate handshakes that Puppyface and the other guys shared before. Taylor looks a little surprised but muddles through it. "Y'all have fun," he says to Anabelle and comes over to Raqia. "Ready to go?" he murmurs.

It appears Taylor does indeed like carrot cake. Anabelle is beaming next to him.

Raqia nods. "Where are we going?" she asks.

He slides an arm around her waist. "Anywhere you like. I just want to be with you."

"Okay." She smiles as they walk out the front door. "That sounds good."

A brisk north wind blows her hair back over her shoulders. The trees sway and whisper. It's almost time for cuddly sweaters and cold rains and curling up on the couch with a book. Or a wolf. She can smell wood smoke from someone's fireplace chimney, hear the distant calls of birds on the wing. The air is crisp and clear, and whether here or across the street, she understands, finally, she is home.

Book Group Discussion Questions

1. *STRAY* IS SET in an obviously fantastical environment, yet it bears some resemblance to our own. What features of the world of Animal Affinities echo real life? What struggles that the characters face in this story could be issues real people in our own lives struggle with?

2. To be "other" is, very simply, to be different from the people around you in a way that causes you to feel set apart. This marker of difference, or

"otherness," is typically imposed rather than adopted: essentially, a person who feels "othered" is not usually othered by choice. In what ways is Raqia made to feel like an other in her community? In what ways does she belong?

3. Animal affinities have no more ultimate meaning than eye color, hair color, height, or other physical characteristics. Why do you think the characters have ascribed such importance to what they are and whether a person has them? Does being a Plain One have to be a bad thing? Why or why not?

4. All teens go through dramatic physical transitions. How do these transformations affect our sense of self-worth at that age? How have those impressions changed in adulthood? How might animal affinities adjust the value we place on our physical attributes?

5. Animal affinities, just like certain skills, traits, or maturity, develop at different times for different people as they come of age. How do we cope with changes happening out of sync with our friends or loved ones? What's the difference between outgrowing a relationship and having a relationship that is simply experiencing growing pains?

6. Raqia and Anabelle have been friends for a long time. How is the strength of any friendship challenged by shifts in a person's perspective over the years? What about as a person's perspective changes with the development of animal affinities? How does the power of friendship overcome (or fail to overcome) the growth of individuals in one direction or another?

7. In what ways do we navigate changes in any of the relationships in our own lives? How do we sometimes fail? How are we sometimes successful?

8. What do you imagine the ramifications would be for harming or killing someone's pet in a world where people have animal affinities? What if this pet had nothing to do with their affinity? What could be a case for and a case against there being any consequences for such an action?

9. The characters in this story have a carnivorous diet. Are there ramifications of this when living in a world where people have animal characteristics as part of their humanity? Why or why not?

10. Eddie invites Raqia to take a leadership role among his group of friends. What do you anticipate will happen if Raqia attempts this role? How do you think the power of their particular animal affinities may counterbalance or exacerbate the combination of entrenched sexism and a hormone-driven heterosexual teen dynamic?

11. What role or influence do fantastical affinities such as centaurs, manticores, and phoenixes have in the spectrum of animal affinities? Why or how might they exist in a world with affinities to ordinary animals such as wolves, owls, and giraffes?

12. If you could have an animal affinity, what would you want it to be? What advantages would it give you? How might it cause difficulty in your life?

13. How much of our behavior is part of our inherited characteristics (our nature) rather than what we learn (how we are nurtured)? What role does instinct play in our choices? Can we control our natural impulses? What does it cost to do so? If we had animal affinities, how might we exercise self-control over those affinities to make life meaningful?

Essay on Respect

I was asked to give a speech to the members of my school community on the subject of respect. Our school goes from PreK through 12th grade, so my audience was going to be very large and would range in age from four years old to grandparent. What follows is what I said to my school community that morning.

Good morning. Thank you for inviting me here to speak about our core value of respect. This morning I'd like to tell you all a story.

When I was seven years old, my mother and my grandmother began teaching me how to cook. My grandmother, whom I called Taita because that's the Levantine Arabic word for Grandma, would come over to our house every Saturday, and she and my mother would spend the day making Lebanese food. When I was seven, they decided it was time I start learning how to do it, too. Now, learning to make Lebanese food is not a quick or simple process. There are no written recipes involved, and it takes most of the day; for example, making a batch of pita bread takes about five hours.

And while we made the food, Taita and my mother told me stories. I learned about how our family's recipes had evolved over the generations, brought from Tripoli and Zouth-n-Kayek, from Bekfiya and Beirut, then to San Antonio and finally to Houston. I learned about the many people in my family who'd made this food before me and what their lives were like. I learned Taita had not had to measure a single ingredient since the age of twelve because she'd made cooking for her large family a big part of her life's work.

And while I mixed ground lamb and onions and pine nuts to make kibbe, or stuffed grapeleaves and yellow squash with lamb and rice, I learned I was part of a rich and beautiful tradition. In learning to make this food, I came to understand my place in my family, in my culture, and—I thought—in the world.

One Monday morning, I decided to take some of the delicious Lebanese food I'd made to school with me for lunch. At that time, schools didn't worry about food allergies, so my second-grade classmates and I all traded food in the lunchroom every day. As soon as everyone sat down at a table, the negotiations would begin:

"I'll trade you a ham-and-cheese for your cupcake."

"If I give you my Cheetos, can I have half your peanut butter and jelly sandwich?"

Things like that.

Well, I'd packed my Wonder Woman lunchbox that morning with some of my favorite foods, foods I was proud of, that I had made myself while participating in my family's heritage. I started with the cookies. I asked, "Would anyone like a ma'amoul? No? I also have graybeh." They looked at me like I was speaking Martian, not Arabic. So I switched to the English names: "How about a date finger?"

There was similar disinterest for my entrée, spinach pies. These are warm hand-held pies made of soft bread and filled with spinach and onions and lemon, and they were my favorite lunch. I'd brought two because I was sure someone else would want one.

Most of the reactions to my lunch ranged from unkindness—my classmates calling my food weird and gross—to polite distaste. They declined to sample any of it, much less trade me their Oreos for it, even though none of them had ever tried these foods before. And I felt torn: on the one hand, it looked like I was going to get to enjoy it all myself without having to share it; on the other hand, my seven-year-old sense of identity had become wrapped up in this food, in the communal process of creating it, and in what it meant to be Lebanese and to be part of my family. This food represented my culture, my accomplishments, and who I was as a person. So when my friends said my lunch was weird and gross, it felt like they were saying *I* was weird and gross.

Now, I mentioned that some of them were polite. They didn't insult my lunch, but they didn't want to try it, either. Politeness *looks* like respect, but it is not the *same* as respect. If you look up respect in the dictionary, you'll see it means "to consider something in high regard." To respect someone or something means that you think that person or thing is important and has value. If you look up politeness in the dictionary, you'll find it means "marked by an *appearance* of deference or courtesy." Some of my classmates politely declined to share my food, but it felt like they didn't want to share in my experience, in who I was.

I did have one brave friend who, after she saw me eating my lunch, decided she would try it. She asked me if she could have a graybeh, which is a thick butter-and-sugar cookie with half a walnut embedded in the top, and I gave her one, and she liked it. Then I broke a ma'amoul – which is a sweet crumbly pastry filled with spiced dates and rolled in sugar – and gave her half. She liked that as well. She even had part of a spinach pie and declared it to be "actually pretty good." She shared her chocolate bar with me, too. That one friend showed me respect by appreciating what I had to offer.

I want to paraphrase something my wise friend Christa Forster once told me, which is that all the things which make up who we are—our memories, our traditions, what we like or value—these things which make us unique and special are all golden. And when we share what matters to us with each other, we share that gold. And when we accept other people with an open mind and an open heart, when we celebrate what makes each other unique and special, we become richer. Just like my friend in second grade who discovered a whole new cuisine she liked eating, when we respect other people by accepting them, we gain a richer understanding and appreciation of them and what they have to offer, and also of the world.

Thank you so much for your attention today. Have a wonderful school year.

Angélique Jamail
August 23, 2019

Acknowledgements

T HERE ARE MANY, MANY people who deserve acknowledgement any time I step foot on the path to publication. For *Stray*, I most especially want to thank. . .

. . .Ynes at Memento Vivere Press, who loved the Animal Affinities stories as much as I did and who is helping to make these books, and the whole series, the gems they are. . .

. . .my editor Alex, who is awesome to work with and whose guidance on this manuscript made it so much better. . .

. . .Maria and Rue, whose artwork for this series has been glorious. . .

. . .David and Sarah, my write-or-dies without whom I could not possibly be the writer I am, and without whom I probably would've leaped from the Writer Brain ™ ledge long ago. . .

. . .Aaron, Kara, Charlotte, and Sarah, beta readers who gave me such valuable feedback on the last draft before it went to copy editing. . .

. . .Grant, for answering my random text messages about whether my memory of colloquial French was completely outdated. . .

. . .Derek, whose musings on the world of Animal Affinities are insightful, entertaining, and so helpful when I'm trying to develop new premises for more books. . .

. . .Paula, Christa, Nadine, Melissa, Scott, Kara, Courtney, and Michael, for being completely excellent in general, and for being such good listeners and/or company in particular. . .

. . .Aaron and Han and Liam, who are the stars in my sky, mysterious and precious and vital. . .

. . .you, my readers, because without you, I'm just someone scribbling in her diary and living inside her imagination. I prefer being a published author, so thank you also for making it possible.

Angélique Jamail is a Lebanese-American author whose work has appeared in numerous publications, including *Synkroniciti, Equinox, New Reader Magazine, Waxwing, The Milk of Female Kindness, Femmeliterate, Literary Mama,* and many others. The first time she read one of her stories to an audience was in fourth grade; it was a character-building experience. Her other books include *A Narrowing Path* (fiction, Memento Vivere Press) and *The Sharp Edges of Water* (poetry, Odeon Press). Her work has been nominated for Best Small Fictions and Best of the Net (for essay), has been a finalist for the New Letters Prize in Poetry, and has won various essay contests. She serves on the Board of Directors for Mutabilis Press and is the Director of Creative Writing at The Kinkaid School. She's also the creator of the popular zine *Sonic Chihuahua* and a member of SFWA.